WIPED OUT IN WIMBLEDON

Cassie Coburn Mystery #10

SAMANTHA SILVER

Chapter 1

A lot of perks came with being friends with Violet Despuis, but this was the best one I'd experienced so far. Thanks to her solving a case for one of the richest men in London, the owner of one of the major sponsors of the Wimbledon tennis tournament, we were currently being whisked to the top of one of London's hottest bars, the location of the biggest pretournament event.

"I hope Serena Williams is going to be there," I gushed as our taxi sped toward the venue. "And Naomi Osaka. They're both so incredible. The way Naomi took time off for her mental health when she needed it was great. Even though they tried to punish her. I think this shift in society, that athletes need to be allowed to rest too, is a good one. But of course, it's tennis. You don't care."

A small smile curled the corner of Violet's

mouth. "And why do you think I would not appreciate tennis?"

"Because I've never seen you show the least bit of appreciation for any sports whatsoever," I said with a shrug.

"Ah, *mais le tennis*, it is different. It is a beautiful game. The strength and agility required to play it, combined with the mental prowess in seeing the play and the opportunities to score a point—they are unparalleled in any other sport if you ask me. It is the perfect game, and I do enjoy it. I have been known to attend Roland-Garros in the past," she replied, referring to the stadium in Paris in which the French Open was played.

"Well, thank you for inviting me along with you," I said as I looked down at my dress. I hadn't had a reason to wear a fancy cocktail dress in a while, and this was one of my favorites. It was an A-line emerald chiffon dress that complemented my red hair beautifully, with a V-neck that showed off just enough cleavage. I'd paired it with a gold clutch and matching heels. I felt totally ready to mingle with some of the best tennis players in the world.

Okay, who was I kidding? Of course I wasn't. They were some of the world's biggest sports stars. But I was excited about it.

"I have seen you watch the tennis on television, so I knew you would enjoy this," Violet said with a smile. "It should be an interesting night."

Little did she know just how right she was.

THE TAXI PULLED UP TO THE BUILDING KNOWN AS the Gherkin for its resemblance to a pickle—that was the PG nickname everyone went with, anyway —and Violet and I stepped out. Wearing a simple black dress that showed off her figure, with her long brown hair streaming down her back, accented with diamonds in her ears and on her fingers, and wearing silver shoes, Violet looked as stunning as I'd ever seen her.

The two of us entered the Gherkin and took the elevator to the top floor, where the Iris Bar over-looked all of London. The bar had been rented out entirely by Jeremy Flagstaff, the billionaire owner of Flagstaff International, a company with fingers in virtually every pie—banking, sports teams, musical productions, real estate, and more. Jeremy had made his initial money in the eighties, when he invested in a couple of musical productions in London's West End that ended up making millions of dollars and being shown all around the world, including on Broadway in the States. He then rein-vested that money and built himself an empire, and he now sat somewhere around number ten on the list of the world's richest men.

We showed our identification to the security guards at the elevators then rose to the thirty-fourth floor, where we exited and took a different elevator to get to the thirty-ninth floor. The Iris Bar was located in the very top of the building. I'd been here before but never to the peak, which offered a 360-degree view past the triangular support frames that wove their way up the entire skyscraper. I looked upward into the London sky. Twilight was just beginning—it was a little after nine o'clock—and it wouldn't be long before the deepening blue would turn to black. Or at least, as close to black as it ever got in London. The streetlights always cast a soft orange glow into the sky.

There were about a hundred and fifty people between me and the windows that offered a gorgeous view over London. Everyone was dressed to the nines, with waiters and waitresses walking past, carrying flutes of champagne.

Was that Ash Barty walking past? My eyes widened as I realized that yes, it was.

"Come on, Cassie," Violet said, nudging my elbow slightly.

We stepped away from the elevator and were immediately greeted by a waiter, who offered us glasses of champagne. I took one, but Violet smiled and shook her head at the waiter.

"Let me guess: you don't want the alcohol to go to your head and kill any of your brain cells."

"It is true, I generally do not drink alcohol for that reason. But no. In this particular instance, it is because we do not know the origins of the drink. The waiter has been going around, handing out flutes of champagne to anyone who asks. Who is to know what was slipped into one of the drinks without him noticing?"

I raised my eyebrows at my friend. "Really? You think there's a risk of something like that happening here? Tonight?"

"If you have learned anything from me, it should be that just because one has or is surrounded by money does not mean they are less likely to become the victim of a crime. In fact, I would offer that the opposite is true."

"Okay, you have a point there."

"So no. I will not be drinking the champagne. But by all means, do not let my own hesitance stop you."

"I won't, because that's overdoing it. No one is going to poison a random glass of champagne here tonight."

I took a sip of my champagne, keeping my eyes locked with Violet's the entire time. She rolled hers at me, and I laughed.

"Come," Violet said. "There is Jeremy. You have not met him yet, correct?"

"Yeah, that's right. I was working a double shift when you solved that case for him. It was a quick one, wasn't it?"

"Indeed. But just because something was quick did not make it less complex. It was a very interesting case. The thief who was stealing from Jeremy's company did an excellent job of covering their tracks. But I was smarter."

I smiled at Violet's complete lack of humility and followed her through the crowd. I was pretty sure I caught another glimpse of Ash Barty, the Australian superstar, talking to somebody near one of the arches of greenery that dotted the space, giving the industrial feel of the bar a more homey touch.

We passed the bar, done up in an art deco style, and pushed past partygoers until we reached a man surrounded by people. In his fifties, maybe early sixties, Jeremy Flagstaff oozed personality from every pore. He was of average height, with a shaggy mess of auburn hair. His blue eyes glimmered with excitement as he spoke excitedly to the man in front of him, the champagne in his flute sloshing around as he gestured. Whatever he said got a reaction; the other man laughed good-naturedly before clapping him on the shoulder, saying something, and walking off.

Violet took that opportunity to step forward, and I followed her.

"Jeremy," she greeted him.

"Ah, Violet," the man replied. "My favorite Frenchwoman. How go things in the investigative world? I'm so glad you could make it."

"I wanted to introduce you to my friend and often associate, Cassie Coburn," Violet said.

I stepped forward, holding my hand out for Jeremy to shake.

His grip was firm, and he looked me in the eyes

as he said, "Cassie. It's nice to meet you. I'm sure I've read about your cases with Violet in the news. Very impressive."

"Thank you very much," I replied. "It's nice to meet you as well."

"Listen, Violet," Jeremy said, turning back to her. "I don't mean to bring up work on a night like this, but is there any chance you could come by my office at some point tomorrow? I've got a little situation with someone going on. Nothing too bad, just business stuff, but I'd like to hire you so you can look into a few things for me. Would that be all right?"

"*Bien sur,*" Violet replied. "I will be there. Can it wait until the morning? If you would like, I am certain we can find somewhere private to speak of the matter now."

"Oh no, I'm sure that isn't necessary," Jeremy replied with a wave of his hand. "Tomorrow morning will be more than fine. Tonight isn't for working. It's for enjoying ourselves and celebrating the best that the tennis world has to offer. Andy Murray just texted me; he should be here any minute. I'm going to try and convince him to have a go at darts against Raffa. That should be a blast. Although I'm not sure they have a darts board here. Maybe we'll do a push-ups contest instead."

"That sounds fun," I said with a chuckle.

"I'm just an old man blabbing on," Jeremy said with a wink. "Go, meet some people far more interesting than me. Enjoy yourself."

I laughed and thanked Jeremy again then headed off to find Violet, who had disappeared. I ended up strolling through the crowd, playing spot the tennis player.

My knee, which acted up less and less often these days, twinged slightly. I knew why. I was in a room full of athletes, feeling inferior because my body wasn't in peak physical condition. Yes, it was true that most of the time, I was able to live my life normally, but the fact was that my ACL had been reconstructed after I was hit by a car, along with a number of other injuries to my soft tissue. I would never be in peak physical condition like these tennis players, nor would I ever master the profession I'd chosen, as my dream of being a surgeon had been taken from me before it had even started.

I found myself heading away from the crowd, toward one of the interior walls, as I tried to deal with my emotions. Honestly, it had been a long time since I'd felt this way. I had made a lot of progress on my own mental health. I had a career in medicine that I enjoyed now, even though it wasn't surgery, and I saw a therapist a couple times a month.

I was definitely going to bring this up the next time I saw Fiona.

"Are you just as uncomfortable with small talk as I am?" a voice said next to me, and I found myself staring at Emily Connors, the Canadian phenom who had climbed the ranks of the WTA after winning the last two Grand Slams. Only eighteen years old, she was quickly being compared to the Williams sisters. Standing around five foot ten, with an athletic frame, Emily wore a long, backless dress that showed off her muscular figure, and her blond ponytail draped over the front of her shoulder. Her gray eyes scanned my face with curiosity as if wondering whether I would be a friend.

"Well, it's not so much the small talk as intimidation from being around all you amazingly athletic women," I said with a nervous chuckle. "And I'm not really used to this feeling. Normally, I'm actually quite confident. But I guess there's a lot in my brain I need to unpack."

"I get you. Honestly, a part of me feels the same way. I know I've won a couple of tournaments, but it doesn't feel real. Only a few years ago, I was at home in Toronto, sitting on the couch, watching Wimbledon on TV, rooting for some of the biggest names in tennis. And now I'm here myself, playing against and beating the women I used to jump up and down cheering for. It doesn't feel real. Sorry. I didn't mean to dump on you." Then a horrified expression crossed Emily's face. "You're not a reporter, are you?"

"No," I said with a kind smile. "Don't worry. I'm a doctor. Here as a plus-one. I'm Cassie."

"Emily. It's nice to meet you. So you don't actually know Jeremy yourself?"

"I just met him. He seems like a nice guy. How about you?"

"I met him at the French Open last month. You're right, he does seem nice. My agent has a meeting with him; we're organizing sponsorships, apparently."

"Oh, congratulations!"

A flush crawled up Emily's neck. "Thank you. I really appreciate it. This whole thing has really blown up for me. I don't quite get the magnitude of it yet."

"No, but you will. And you'll come to appreciate it. You're living out your dreams, aren't you?"

A grin spread across Emily's face. "I am, yeah. It feels awesome, but at the same time, I constantly want to pinch myself to see if I wake up."

"That's the best kind, isn't it? The one that's really happening to you."

"No kidding. I don't want to sound ungrateful, because I'm not at all. This is the life I've been dreaming of since I was a little girl. It's just all happened so fast."

"Definitely."

"So, are you American?"

"I am. I grew up in San Francisco. Is this your first time in England?"

"No, I've been here before, for tournaments. You seem familiar though." Emily squinted at me for a moment then snapped her fingers. "I've got it.

You're the woman who works with that famous detective. Violet Despuis."

I laughed. "Yup, that's me. She's the reason I'm here tonight; we came together."

"Oh, I didn't realize the two of you were a couple. I'm sorry."

"We're not. I'm straight, and Violet is… well, a robot." I genuinely had no idea as to what Violet's preference was for a romantic partner. I'd never seen her so much as flirt with anybody unless it was to coerce information from them.

Emily chuckled. "Fair enough."

"Violet helped Jeremy out with something a couple of months ago, but I was working then and wasn't involved in that case."

"What kind of medicine do you practice?"

"Emergency."

"That's really cool. What's the grossest thing you've ever seen?" Emily asked, her eyes lighting up.

I laughed at her youthful enthusiasm before telling her about the machine that basically acted as a pressure washer to remove stones from under people's skin when they fell on their bikes. That one usually got a squirmy reaction from people.

Emily and I continued chatting for a little while. She was nice, and I liked her. We spoke about tennis, I ended up telling her my story, and we discussed how life could take us to unexpected places.

Suddenly, there came a crash from another part

of the bar. The sound of shattering glass told me it was likely one of the waiters had dropped a tray of champagne, but the ruckus that continued afterward was too great.

"What's going on over there?" Emily asked, frowning.

"I don't know. Let's go have a look."

The two of us rushed over and joined the hordes of people trying to see what had happened. Then I heard the call.

"Is anyone here a doctor?" someone yelled.

"Cassie," I heard Violet's voice say.

I immediately began forcing my way past onlookers. When I reached the front of the crowd, I saw Jeremy Flagstaff on the ground, surrounded by gaping onlookers, his eyes staring upward. I immediately dropped to his side and tried to get a pulse, but there was nothing. I tried CPR, but it was quickly obvious that it was too late. He was dead.

"We need to get everyone out of here," I said to Violet quietly. "And call the police."

Violet nodded. "I smell it too. Cyanide."

Someone had poisoned one of the richest men in England.

Chapter 2

The next few minutes were chaos personified. Luckily, given the high-profile status of many of the attendees, there was plenty of security in attendance, and the guards were able to effectively clear the floor within moments, while Violet immediately began investigating.

I looked at the body. It showed clear signs of cyanide poisoning, although the pathologist's report would confirm that later. Jeremy's champagne flute had shattered on the floor where he dropped it. Shards of glass lay near his feet, and sticky drops of the fluid shimmered on the ground nearby.

"When the police come, they'll need to test that," I said to Violet, motioning to the champagne. "Be sure to tell them."

"I will," Violet replied with a nod. She shot me a look. "Very low odds, you said."

"Of course, the *one time* someone's champagne is

poisoned at a party I attend, we had to have that conversation."

I looked around the room. It was amazing how still it seemed now with only the head of security, Violet, and me here on the floor.

Violet turned to him. "Tell me about tonight. Who was here with Jeremy? Did you notice anything in particular that stood out?"

"No," the man replied, all business. "Mr. Flagstaff arrived around seven o'clock, before most of the other guests. I asked him whether he had private security with him, and he told me he did not. He spent the majority of the night speaking with other attendees. I don't think I saw him alone for a moment, although I spent much of the night out of sight of him. We have taken the other attendees downstairs to the restaurant, where we're keeping them until the police arrive."

"Good. You have taken contact information for all of them?"

"I have my staff doing that now."

Before Violet had a chance to respond, the sound of footsteps on the stairs leading to the bar reached our ears, and we turned to see two detectives arrive, followed by a couple of uniformed officers.

The detectives were both men. One appeared to be in his late twenties. He was tall and lanky with close-cut blond hair and a curious air about him. The other was older, in his forties at least, with a bit of a beer belly. He strutted around like a man who knew he could go anywhere. His brown hair was flattened to his forehead with too much gel, and he had over two spots where he'd obviously nicked himself shaving that morning.

"Violet Despuis," the older one said, obviously displeased to see her here. "I should have known."

"And what exactly do you mean by that, DCI Fletcher?"

"I mean that whenever bodies pop up, you always seem to be involved somehow."

"That is a strange way of thanking me, for I tend to solve your cases for you, but I will take it."

"You do not solve the cases *for* me. You take advantage of an overworked and underpaid police force, and you build your own celebrity based off our hard work. Now, what happened here tonight?"

"We were attending a party held by Jeremy Flagstaff, formerly a private client of mine. It is to celebrate Wimbledon. Twenty-seven minutes ago, Jeremy collapsed and was dead nearly instantly. Of course, the pathology report will determine exactly what happened, but given the symptoms and the smell of almonds, I suspect cyanide poisoning."

DCI Fletcher approached the body and sniffed. "I don't smell almonds."

"Well, the ability to smell the bitter almond residue of hydrogen cyanide is genetic," Violet said. "You may not be able to detect it, but that does not mean it isn't there."

DCI Fletcher scowled. "Are you saying I'm genetically inferior?"

"Perhaps you do not want me to answer that question directly. It is not a matter of superiority or inferiority but simple fact."

"It was a single mutation, wasn't it?" the other detective asked. "That turned off the production of the toxin in wild almonds and allowed humans to cultivate and enjoy sweet almonds without immediately suffering an incredibly painful death?"

"That is correct," Violet said approvingly. "What is your name?"

"Er, DCI Emmett Johnson," the man replied nervously, glancing over at DCI Fletcher, who was obviously annoyed.

"Who cares about all that stupid science stuff anyway? We're here to solve a murder."

"And you might be more successful if you bothered to pay attention to any of that 'stupid science stuff,' as you call it," Violet replied.

"Are you telling me how to do my job?"

"Yes. You are obviously incapable of seeing the importance of science in crime solving yourself."

"Okay, then get out of here. I let you stay as a courtesy, but I need the officers to secure the area until the crime scene unit arrives. You can wait downstairs along with everyone else."

I raised my eyebrows at Violet, who just smiled and stood up.

"Yes, we wouldn't want you to use the most

valuable asset you have here. Not a smart officer like you."

DCI Fletcher scowled at Violet, but as we walked past DCI Johnson, he offered us a nervous smile.

The two of us went downstairs to the restaurant area, which had been closed for the night due to the party. Immediately, the manager strode over to us. He was a heavyset man in his forties, dressed in a suit, his brow lined with a thin layer of sweat.

"The police are here?" he asked her. "I thought I saw them go up."

"Yes," Violet replied.

"Good. Good. That poor man. I can't believe it. What happened?"

"We're not sure yet," Violet replied. "Can you recount to us the logistics of this night? I am Violet Despuis, the famous detective, and I will be taking it upon myself to solve this case."

"Of course. Jeremy Flagstaff rented this entire place himself, and he brought in everything: his own staff, his own drinks, his own food. I'm the only person here tonight who actually works here, because I wanted to make sure everything was running smoothly and that his staff had someone to go to if they had any questions. I believe he owns the company that provided the catering. Flagstaff Catering."

I resisted the urge to snort. Yes, that was a pretty safe assumption.

"Did you see Flagstaff?"

"Not in the last hour or so. I spoke to him early in the evening. Nice bloke. But I was working predominantly behind the scenes. This wasn't my night. I appreciate that. Every time I saw him, he was surrounded by people. Obviously, he was popular. So no, I didn't see him recently. But my head of security is getting contact information from everyone who's in here now. Would you like a copy of that list?"

"That would be excellent, thank you," Violet said. "Do you have security footage?"

"We do. Would you like to see it? Normally, we'd require a warrant, but given the exceptional situation…" The manager trailed off. "I just can't allow you to remove the footage from the premises."

"We understand completely," Violet replied.

The manager motioned for us to follow him. As we did so, I looked over the crowd of party attendees. The happy, optimistic vibe of the party from only a few minutes earlier was now very subdued. Most people were sitting at the empty restaurant tables. Emily was in a corner by herself, on her phone. The man I'd seen clap Jeremy on the shoulder earlier was in another corner, also on his phone, his thumb and index finger pressed into the bridge of his nose.

One of the tennis players was meditating, and a couple of others were obviously doing their best to relax as much as possible. I couldn't blame them;

the tournament started tomorrow. Some of them were likely playing.

"You should let the tennis players go back to their hotels," Violet said, echoing my thoughts. "They will be tired. It is not as though we are incapable of contacting them at a later date."

"Right," the manager said as if he'd only just realized the same thing. "That's a good idea. I'll show you to the security footage then run it past the police."

He led us into the back room of the kitchen and into a smaller office where the administrative tasks were obviously taken care of. The room was the size of a janitor's closet, barely large enough for the three of us to stand side by side.

The computer at the center of the plain wooden desk was surrounded by columns of documents, and it sat like a shrine encircled by a paper temple.

"Here," the manager said, clicking away at the computer for a minute. "This is the program. I trust you to figure it out for yourself."

"Thank you. We will be fine," Violet said.

The manager nodded and left.

Violet squeezed into the little chair and began tapping away at the screen while I looked over her shoulder. "I guess it would be too much to ask to hope that we get video footage of someone slipping cyanide into his champagne, huh?"

"It is always an avenue that must be explored. I have come across a number of exceptionally stupid criminals in my time. It is always possible that this is one of them."

"Fingers crossed," I muttered as Violet began scanning through the available camera options.

London was the land of CCTV. Sometimes, it felt as if there wasn't an inch of this city that didn't fall under video surveillance, but in this case, it was actually pretty useful. It didn't take long before Violet found the camera that had had Jeremy Flagstaff in frame. He was in the center of the floor, facing the camera, speaking with someone I didn't recognize.

"Okay, so keep going forward until he collapses," I said. "From there, we can rewind the tape and see who he spoke to after getting his last glass of champagne."

Violet nodded and tapped away with the mouse. The footage jumped forward until eventually, I saw myself bent over Jeremy's dead body, trying to find a pulse.

Violet then rewound the footage slowly until we saw what we wanted.

Jeremy had been speaking with Ash Barty, and when they split up, he walked out of frame. Violet checked the other angles, and we found him at the bar. He said something to the bartender, who laughed, pulled out a glass, and dug under the counter for a bottle of champagne. The bartender uncorked the bottle then filled Jeremy's glass. Jeremy took it, left a bill on the table, and walked off to chat with some more people.

"Well, the bartender's out," I said. "We had a perfect view of him pouring that flute, and I didn't see him slip anything into it. Did you?"

"No," Violet said. "I agree, it was not him. Now, we follow Jeremy's glass of champagne after this."

Chapter 3

J eremy wandered off to the left and was quickly stopped by someone. I recognized the head even from the back. This was another famous tennis player, who just went by the name El. His birth name was Elton John, as his parents were huge fans of the singer and thought they would honor their son with his name. Unfortunately, when it turned out he was an incredible tennis player, it became a bit confusing, and Elton decided to shorten his name to El. Nicknamed Racketman, El had a wiry frame that towered over Jeremy. His body blocked out all view of the champagne, and whatever they were talking about, the conversation was heated.

I couldn't see El's face, but I could make out Jeremy's. He held a smile the entire time, but it was tight, forced. It was the kind of smile people go with when they don't want to get into a fight in public, but they're completely disagreeing with the person across from them.

"I don't think Racketman is happy about something," I said to Violet.

She nodded. "*Oui*. You are correct. I would like to know what it is that El is unhappy with. The Flagstaff group is one of his major sponsors. The two of them are linked in business. We will have to speak with him."

I watched the screen as El grabbed Jeremy by the arm. Jeremy pulled back slightly, his eyes widening in surprise. I watched his mouth as he spoke to El.

"Can you read those lips?" I asked Violet, squinting at the screen.

"Yes. Jeremy tells El that they can speak about this in the morning, that it is not what he thinks."

"Interesting. I wonder what's going on there."

"We will find out when we speak with El. He would have been distracting enough that he could have poisoned the drink during that conversation."

"I agree."

El left, but before Jeremy had a chance to do anything else, another man walked up to him. I recognized this one; he was the man Jeremy had been speaking to before I was introduced to him.

"Do you know who this is?" I asked Violet.

"Flagstaff's business partner, Sid Miller."

"Business partner? I didn't realize he had someone else."

"I bet you didn't realize Bernie Taupin wrote most of Elton John's songs either," Violet said to me with a wink.

"What? Really? He didn't write them all himself?"

"No. Sometimes, when there is a genius with unparalleled charisma, it is better to have him be the face of the company and to have the other person work everything from the shadows. That is the relationship between Flagstaff and Miller. Everyone knows the name and face of Jeremy Flagstaff, but Sid Miller is an extraordinarily intelligent man, and many people in the know believe him to be the true brains behind the operation. I personally believe that to be rubbish. Having met Flagstaff, I know he is quite intelligent himself. But I can certainly believe that Miller does much of the work behind the scenes."

I looked at the screen. The two of them were deep in conversation. This time, Jeremy wasn't as obviously upset as he had been while speaking with El, but the firm line of his mouth told me this wasn't a pleasant conversation either. The two of them huddled together, heads close.

"Can you make out anything they're saying?" I asked Violet.

She shook her head. "No. I haven't got a clue."

It soon became evident that we weren't going to get anything from this. However, there had been ample opportunity to poison Jeremy.

Eventually, Sid left, scowling slightly, and I had to wonder what had been going on between the two businessmen that led to such acrimony. Of course, it could have been a million different things. But was one of those things important enough to kill Flagstaff over?

The two men did business deals worth millions. It wouldn't have surprised me one bit.

Next, a woman I didn't recognize came by to say hello. "Do you know who she is?" I asked Violet.

"One of the tennis players, from France. Claire Saint-Etienne. She's not ranked very highly and will likely see an exit in the first or second round."

The conversation she had with Jeremy was quick, and this time, his smile seemed genuine.

"He is thanking her for the kind words," Violet said. "He is wishing her luck in the tournament. It does not appear that there is any bad blood between them. In fact, I would not be surprised if they had never met before this."

"Okay, so there's probably no motive there. Still, it's good to know."

Violet nodded. "And this man, on the other hand, does not appear to know what politeness means."

I scowled as I watched the screen. One of the most famous tennis players in the world, Kristof Mayer, pushed through the crowd and practically shoved Claire Saint-Etienne out of the way in his effort to get to Jeremy.

"Well, it's good to see that the reality fits his reputation," I said dryly, shaking my head.

Claire looked surprised when she saw Kristof then hurried out of the way.

Kristof Mayer was the current bad boy of men's tennis. Ranked number two in the world, he was the best tennis player to ever come out of Austria, but he was as well known for his temper and his antics on the court as he was for his play. He regularly broke tennis rackets when he made a bad play, yelled at the umpires, and had once even thrown a ball at a ball boy he thought wasn't doing his job properly.

Basically, the guy was a piece of work that people put up with because he was so good at tennis. I hated that sort of person. Being the best in the world at something didn't mean they had the right to be horrible to everyone else they came into contact with.

Kristof was yelling at Jeremy about something, no question.

"He was not subtle, Kristof," Violet said. "I was standing about twenty meters away, and even I could hear that he was yelling at Jeremy. He told Jeremy that he was being screwed over by his company and that he wasn't going to let this stand. Jeremy would pay. Of course, at the time, I did not think much of this. Kristof has a certain reputation, and it did not surprise me in the least to hear him say such things. However, in hindsight, given that

Jeremy ended up dead, it will be worth investigating further."

"No kidding. It wouldn't surprise me at all if Kristof killed him."

"Wouldn't it?"

"No. Kristof has always had a temper. He's the kind of guy who yells at people and doesn't care about the consequences. You watch tennis. You've seen him break rackets. One time, he even tried to rip the net apart, remember? It was turned into a meme and plastered all over the internet."

"Ah, but that is precisely why I do not believe Kristof is the killer."

"What? That makes no sense. He's shown a propensity for violence."

"Violence, yes. But not all violence is created equal. Every instance you have recounted of Kristof Mayer committing violence involves him snapping in the moment. However, think of how Jeremy was killed."

"With poison slipped into his drink."

"Yes. Whoever wanted him dead planned this ahead of time. They brought the poison to the party. They took their time before approaching him, and they slipped the poison into his drink without his noticing it. It requires a subtle touch that Kristof does not have. No, if he had done this, I would have expected it to be public, violent, and bloody. He would have taken a knife and stabbed the man or something like that. Not this. This is the work of someone more deliberate."

"Okay, I see what you mean. You're right. This crime does require a bit of forethought and subtlety that he doesn't have. He wouldn't have done it. That's too bad though. I was kind of hoping it was him. It's never the awful people that you really want to have be guilty and go to jail."

Violet smiled. "Personally, I would rather the person who actually murdered another human being be the one who goes to jail."

"Sure. I don't disagree. But I'd rather the killer just happen to be the person I didn't like in the first place."

"Well, you cannot always get what you want."

"Thanks, Mick Jagger."

"I do not know who that is."

"Really? You don't know the Rolling Stones, but you know the name of the guy who wrote all of the songs for Elton John?"

Violet shrugged. "I have my interests."

Violet's knowledge base was always so incredibly random.

"Okay," I said. "So, we don't think it was Kristof, as disappointing as that is."

Violet played the tape further. Kristof and Jeremy were arguing. Then Kristof shoved Jeremy, who took a step back, and a couple of security people immediately came over. Kristof was led away, and Jeremy took a sip of his champagne. He looked relaxed for a moment, and then his eyes widened. His features contorted into a look of terror, and then he collapsed. Immediately, Jeremy was surrounded by people and fell out of view of the camera. I knew what happened next.

"It had to be one of them then," I said. "One of the people he spoke to. El, Sid, Claire, or Kristof."

Violet nodded. "It certainly does appear that way. It could also have been Emily Connors. She passed behind Jeremy at one point while he was arguing with Kristof. She could have slipped it into his drink without anyone realizing."

I didn't like to think about the nice young Canadian being a murderer, but I knew it was possible. Sometimes, the killer was the last person we expected.

"I spent the night talking to her. She met Jeremy at the French Open a month ago. If she had a motive, she didn't make it obvious to me."

Violet smiled. "Did you tell her who you were?"

"Yes. She thought we were a couple, actually."

"Well, do you think that if she was going to murder somebody, she would tell you, a person who introduced themselves as a friend to one of the world's most famous detectives, the reason she had for killing a man here tonight?"

"What makes you think she knew who you were? After all, you don't know who Mick Jager is," I teased. "But you're right. I didn't say she didn't do it. I like her. I will say that. But I also know that just because I like someone doesn't mean they're innocent. I know all too well that's not how it works."

"Good. At least now we have our list of suspects. Do you know what Emily was doing?"

"She told me she had to go to the bathroom," I said. "She came back around five minutes later. But given where the bathrooms were, she shouldn't have gone past where Jeremy was standing. That's the wrong way."

"That is interesting," Violet said. "Very interesting. All right. I have seen what we need to see. Tomorrow, we begin interviews. For now, we leave."

"Do you think we're going to get anything else from those two cops?"

"No. They will not be able to help us until they have gotten the pathology report back, and that will not be for days. Besides, we know it was cyanide. It has not been confirmed yet, but the two of us both smelled the bitter almonds. That scent is unmistakable. No, now, we gather as much information as possible. Will you be investigating this along with me?"

"Are you kidding? This is Wimbledon! And one of the most famous businessmen in the world was just murdered. Of course I'm getting involved. But what about you? This case is interesting to *me*, but what's in it for you? It seems kind of boring from an investigative point of view."

"It most certainly is. But then, it has been a

while since I have had a palate cleanser of a case. This one should not be too difficult to solve."

"Why bother then?"

"Because, my dear Cassie, someone attended this party, was likely aware of my presence, and decided to commit a murder anyway. That is an insult to me. Whoever it was should have known I was there and immediately changed their mind and decided to kill Jeremy Flagstaff at another time. The fact that they did it under my nose? Bah. No, they cannot be allowed to get away with it."

I shot Violet a wry smile. "So it's not the fact that a crime was committed but the fact that they dared to commit it under your nose that's the issue?"

"*Oui, c'est ca.*"

I chuckled to myself. Sometimes, Violet had the most ego-driven reasons for investigating a case. "Well, on the bright side, it doesn't sound as if you think it'll be too hard to solve."

"No, I do not think it will be. However, there is nothing left to do tonight. Tomorrow, we speak with our suspects, and after that, we solve the murder."

"Easy as pie."

Chapter 4

The two of us left the office and headed back into the main restaurant area. Most of the patrons who had been there had gone, although DCI Johnson was interviewing Sidney Miller, Jeremy's business partner and one of our main suspects.

Violet motioned for me to join her near him. Johnson glanced over at us and offered a smile but didn't tell us to get lost or anything.

"Can you think of anyone who would have wanted Jeremy dead?" DCI Johnson asked. This was obviously the beginning of the interview.

"Yes. Kristof Mayer," Sid replied. He glanced over at us. "You've already brought in Violet Despuis? Good. I want Jeremy's killer found."

"What was the beef between Mayer and Flagstaff?" I asked. "They argued tonight."

"It was over sponsorship. Our company owns a majority stake in Victory Shoes, the trainer company. Mayer was our highest-profile athlete, but Jeremy had decided to cancel his contract. He told him earlier today, when the two of them had lunch. I think Jeremy expected that Mayer wouldn't show up tonight, but he did."

"How much was the contract worth?" DCI Johnson asked, scribbling everything Sid was saying into a notepad.

"Seventy-two million pounds," Sid replied, and my eyes widened.

I let out a low whistle. "Yeah, that would be enough to kill someone over. Even someone as rich as Mayer."

"Why were you cancelling the contract?" Violet asked.

Sid shrugged. "We'd had enough of his antics. It was getting tiresome. When you sign an athlete to your label, you expect them to meet a certain professional standard. Yes, he's an excellent tennis player. But what does that matter when nobody respects him due to his actions on and off the court? So we used the morals clause in his contract to terminate it early. He wasn't pleased, obviously. In fact, Jeremy called me later that day. He said Kristof threatened to kill him."

"Did Jeremy take that threat seriously?" DCI Johnson asked. "Maybe report it to the police?"

Sid shook his head. "No, not at all. Jeremy knew Kristof. Knew the kind of hot-headed man he was. He figured Kristof would cool down after a while.

He certainly never took the threat seriously. If the police were called every time Kristof threatened to kill somebody, he'd have a permanent entourage."

"You do realize that's kind of an enormous red flag, right?" I said.

Sid shrugged. "It's just how he is. Or at least, how I thought he was. I never took the threats seriously either. Kristof probably told me he'd kill me at least twice in my life. I never thought anything of it. Of course, now that Jeremy is dead… I still can't believe it."

"I want to go back to the contract," Violet said. "Give me the real reason you are cancelling it."

Sid looked slightly surprised. "I've told you the real reason. We finally had enough of his antics."

Violet shook her head. "You are lying. Kristof Mayer has not been in the news recently for doing anything exceptionally stupid. There is no reason to choose now, in particular, as a time to cancel his contract. That means that something else has happened. You are aware of allegations that will be coming out, will you not? Something he has done that has not yet made it to the public eye?"

Sid glanced down to the floor. "No, nothing like that," he said, but even I could tell he was lying his butt off.

"It is late, and I am tired. I am certain you are as well and that you would enjoy getting to go home. Why don't you just tell me what I need to know now? Because I will find out what it is that Mayer has done. Believe me, I have contacts and networks around the world that run deeper than you could possibly imagine. I have world leaders on speed dial. You think you are well connected? Compared to me you are Robinson Crusoe. And if I have to find out through my networks what he has done, I will ensure that your name is dragged through the mud alongside Mayer's. So, I ask you again. What did Mayer do?"

Sid looked as if he wanted to take on Violet. He opened his mouth to speak, but Violet had a way of taking over a room when she wanted to. She towered over him despite her short stature, and instead of arguing, he cowered slightly, swallowing hard.

"Okay," he finally said, his eyes darting from one face to the other. "But nothing I say here can leave this room. You have to promise me that."

"I cannot make such a promise," DCI Johnson said. "I'm an officer of the law."

"Personally, I only care about who killed Jeremy," Violet replied with a shrug. "The rest, I will leave to the detective inspector. But I recommend you tell us what you know all the same, particularly if you have not committed any crimes."

"Fine," Sid finally said with a sigh. "I knew this was going to end badly. I just knew it. I didn't want Jeremy to nullify the contract before this all came out. I thought the timing would be suspicious. People would realize we knew. And we did know.

Another athlete told us about it. Mayer wouldn't. He's trying to sweep it under the rug. But the fact of the matter is, last month in Berlin, at his practice facility, he got drunk one night and assaulted a woman at a bar. Apparently, she rejected his advances, and he punched her. The bouncers kicked him out, but he knocked one of them out by hitting him over the head with a champagne bottle."

I gasped. "How come this isn't all over the news already?"

"It happened in the VIP section of the club, so there were a very limited number of witnesses, and most were part of his entourage. Mayer went to the club the next day and wrote some hefty checks, which took care of the workers there. Then he wrote a seven-figure check to the woman, and she signed an NDA in exchange. Mayer doesn't think it's ever going to come out."

"And yet you found out about it," DCI Johnson said.

"Yes," Sidney said, nodding profusely. "That's why Jeremy and I met over it. We had to get ahead of it. It's one thing to argue with a referee on the court, but to punch a woman in the face? We can't support that. It's not even about the money. It's about the man's character. We can't be supporting someone like that. Someone who does that. I have daughters. I have to think about them."

"Did you tell the police in Berlin what you learned?" Violet asked.

"No. No, of course not. We decided it was best to keep things quiet, especially after we chose to terminate the contract."

"So you do not want him to be able to assault anyone else, but you will not go to the police to do anything about it for fear of it affecting your company's reputation? He faces no consequences."

"I wouldn't say that the dissolution of his contract with us amounts to *no* consequences," Sid replied. "We did what we thought was best. It wasn't our place to go to the police. Besides, we know what would happen if we did. The woman has signed an NDA. She denies anything happened, Mayer gets his name dragged through the mud, and we get caught up in it because we cancelled his contract and people think we knew and didn't say anything. We didn't want that."

"Yes, you could not possibly do something that would lead to fewer shoes being sold," Violet said dryly.

"Look, it's business. It sucks. I know it does, but that's capitalism. You don't like it? Take it up with Adam Smith. But that's the reality right now. And I'll admit, I didn't want to cancel the contract straight away. But it was a damned-if-you-do, damned-if-you-don't situation. It could blow up in our face if we cancelled it, and it could blow up in our face if we didn't, and what he did came out. So ultimately, when Jeremy suggested we use the morals clause to get rid of him, I agreed. Because it's the better of two bad situations. Believe me, I'm not happy about it either. But now that it's done, this can't get out. It would ruin us if it did. Ruin me, I guess, since Jeremy is dead now. We need everything to continue as normal."

"There's a dead body upstairs. Normal is no longer an option," DCI Johnson said dryly.

"What about you? You said you disagreed with the plan initially?" Violet asked. "We saw you disagreeing with Jeremy tonight. What was your argument about?"

"Look, we were trying to keep it away from everyone. I didn't want news getting out that the two of us were arguing. But our argument had nothing to do with the Mayer situation."

"What was it, then?"

"El. You know, Racketman? Well, Jeremy had the brilliant idea of bringing him onto the brand as well in the aftermath of cancelling Kristof's contract. Of course, we would wait a suitable amount of time before doing so. Personally, I thought it was a bad idea."

"Why?" I asked.

"El is a great athlete, no doubt about it, but he just doesn't have that same presence that Kristof has. That same ability to capture the public. He's too bland. There. I said it. And he has the exact same name as one of the most famous people in England, who's the opposite of bland. When someone talks about Elton John, you think sequined jackets. You think "Candle in the Wind." You think of elaborately decorated pianos and a man who can get the roof at Wimbledon to fly off. You don't think of the tennis player. And I don't mean that to disparage the man. He's one of the best players in the world. It's just that he's got the personality of a slice of white bread, and you can't sell that."

I raised my eyebrows. "So you were trying to convince Jeremy to change his mind."

"And I succeeded too. I told him at the beginning of the night to watch El. Just see how he interacted with people and ask whether that was the kind of man he wanted for our brand. The next time I spoke to Jeremy, just before he died, he told me that I was right. El wasn't suitable for the brand, and he wanted to take the company in another direction. He said we'd find another athlete. We organized to discuss it in the morning."

"That is your story?" Violet asked.

"It's the truth," Sid said, opening his hands. "I'm telling you. Jeremy and I had a good relationship. We knew each other. We started the Flagstaff Group back in the late eighties, when we'd both just come out of Oxford together. I know Jeremy better than I know my own brother. We've been through multiple recessions together, and I didn't murder him. We've had much bigger disagreements than this one. I'm telling you, I had nothing to do with this. Please believe me, so you can move on and find the person who did. Because Jeremy was my best friend in the entire world."

"If you didn't do this, apart from Kristof Mayer, can you think of anyone else who would have?"

Sid ran a hand down his face, and when he pulled it away, it was as if he'd aged fifteen years. The man was obviously struggling tonight. But was it from genuine grief, or was it from the stress of knowing he'd just killed a man and being interrogated by the police about it now?

"I don't know. I really don't. The business was fine. We've had rough times, when I would have had a better answer for you, but we weren't there right now. The economy is doing great. All of the businesses under the Flagstaff umbrella were setting record profits. Deals were being made, and everyone was happy. Well, as much as anyone can be in business. If you'd asked me this same question in 2008, I would have had a different answer for you. I could have named half a dozen people who I thought could have easily killed Jeremy. But no. I don't know. I really don't."

"All right, thank you, Mr. Miller," DCI Johnson said. He turned to Violet. "Do you have any other questions to ask?"

"No, I got what I needed from this conversation," Violet replied.

"Does that mean I can go? I have some calls to make. Our lawyers need to know what happened right away. This is going to affect so many things," Sid said, trailing off.

DCI Johnson motioned for him to leave, then he turned to Violet. "I don't think it was Mayer. The psychology isn't right."

Violet turned to DCI Johnson, curiosity in her eyes. "Why do you say that?"

"Mayer is a hothead. He would have done it on the spot. Whoever did this premeditated the murder."

"Ah, *très bien*," Violet said approvingly. "It is good that you study the criminal mind."

DCI Johnson's face flushed red in the way only an Englishman's could. "Thanks. I find it important, you know? Even if DCI Fletcher doesn't think so."

"DCI Fletcher does not have two brain cells to rub together," Violet replied. "Do not bother yourself with what he believes. You appear to me to be much more intelligent than him. Continue to study the psychology of killers. It will serve you well."

The two of us said goodbye to DCI Johnson and left the building, flagging down a cab to take us back home.

Chapter 5

"I'm guessing it's far too early to ask you what you think about Sid Miller?" I asked with a smile as we sped off.

"You know me too well," Violet replied with a small smile of her own. "Yes. At this time, it is too early to come to any firm conclusions. We still need to interview the others. Still, you never know. This might end up being a more interesting case than it appears at first glance."

"Do you still think Kristof Mayer is innocent?"

"I still believe it is unlikely to be him, but I certainly have not eliminated him as a suspect. That would be foolish. He could very well have done it, and he had a motive. But so did Sid. As much as he played down the nature of the ill will that he felt toward Jeremy, I would not put it past him at all to kill his business partner if he felt it advantageous to him in the long haul."

I nodded. "I agree. Nobody gets *that* rich without being willing to stomp all over anybody who gets in their way. He's worth literally billions of dollars. He might put on a good show, but deep down, he's ruthless. Look at how he handled the situation with Kristof after he found out about the assault. He didn't report it to the police. He didn't do anything to ensure Mayer faced any sort of punishment for his actions. He simply did what was best for his own company and then tried to claim that he cared because he had daughters. No, the guy would do anything."

Violet nodded. "And now, we have to prove whether or not he actually *did* something. But that is for tomorrow. You are available?"

"Sure am. I wouldn't miss this investigation for the world."

Violet smiled. "Well, if we are lucky, it will be solved quickly."

THE TAXI DROPPED US OFF ON ELDON ROAD, AND Violet and I split up, each going to our separate homes. When I arrived, my boyfriend, Jake, was sleeping. Biscuit and Sequoia, our cat and dog, were curled up together on the rug in the living room, so I crawled into bed with Jake and lay awake, staring at the wall, running over all the facts we'd learned tonight in my head.

I must have eventually dozed off, because I woke up to Biscuit, my orange cat, standing on my chest and pawing at my face to wake me up. Someone wanted breakfast.

I crawled out of bed with a groan and found a note from Jake on the counter.

I'm off to work. Saw the news. Glad to see you're okay. Text me if you need anything. Love you. PS. Despite what I'm sure they're both telling you, I've fed Biscuit and Sequoia.

I smiled as I read over the note. I figured Jake would probably be doing the autopsy this morning, as someone like Jeremy Flagstaff would be moved right to the front of the line when it came to making sure this investigation went smoothly.

I checked my phone and saw I had a text from Violet. *We are meeting Elton John at eleven o'clock at his home. He only lives a ten-minute walk from here.*

It was just after nine, so I had a little over ninety minutes to get ready. While the stadium at Wimbledon was located around an hour outside of downtown London, most of the athletes chose to stay at the official partner hotel, which this year was the Park Plaza in Westminster, on the South Bank of the Thames in downtown London.

However, the ones who had homes in London, like El and Andy Murray, usually opted to stay in those homes instead.

I made some eggs on toast for breakfast, put on a pot of coffee, and hopped in the shower. Violet popped by at around a quarter to eleven, and the two of us began the walk down to Allen Road, only a few blocks away.

"I had no idea one of the most famous tennis players in the world lived so close to us," I admitted. "Although I suppose with his schedule, he's probably not home all that often."

"No. And Sid was right about one thing: he's not the kind of attention-seeking man who is always in the news. El is much more reserved. Or so he appears publicly. It will be interesting to see what kind of man he is in person."

We reached his home soon afterward. Frankly, the street was almost indistinguishable from ours, lined with three-story row houses, all painted white. Violet stopped in front of one of the homes with a door painted a simple black. In the single-car driveway at the front sat a BMW 1-series, ideal for city living.

Violet and I climbed the three steps that led to the main entrance, and she knocked firmly on the door. About fifteen seconds later, it opened, and El stood in front of us.

I recognized him instantly from the TV, of course, and the security footage last night, but it was still certainly something to see a man so famous in the flesh. He was tall, at least six foot four, with neatly trimmed brown hair and a freshly shaven jaw. His bright-blue eyes shone in the summer sun, and he was dressed casually in a T-shirt and a pair of jeans, drinking a green smoothie.

"You must be Violet and Cassie," he said, shaking each of our hands. "Come in, come in."

El motioned for us to enter, and he led us into a large kitchen and dining area, which opened through French doors onto an actual backyard, here in downtown London. This property was a total unicorn. A unicorn that probably cost in excess of ten million pounds. Wicker furniture was set up outside, and El motioned for us to sit.

Violet and I took one of the couches, and El leaned back in a chair. "Can I get you anything before we get started? Water? Kombucha?"

"No, thank you," Violet replied. "I would rather get straight to my questions."

"Whatever you need. It was such a shock last night. I still can't believe it really happened. Jeremy Flagstaff, killed at an event like that. Unbelievable."

"Did you know Jeremy well?" Violet asked.

"No. To say hi to, of course. He's the head of one of the biggest sponsors of Wimbledon, so I'd certainly met him before, but I wouldn't say we were close."

"You were spotted on camera with Jeremy a few minutes before his death. What was that conversation about?"

El scowled. "He was ripping me off, that's what it was."

"Oh?" I prompted.

"See, a few days ago, Jeremy comes to me. He says that they're interested in having me become an ambassador for Victory Shoes. He wanted to know what it would take to make that happen."

"Don't you have an agent?" I asked.

"Not for the last year. I felt the last one wasn't getting me good enough deals, so I fired him. I figured I could do it myself. After all, I'm one of the biggest tennis stars in the world. Why wasn't I getting the same kind of sponsorship deal as that idiot, Kristof? Just because he's got a bigger reputation than me? No, that's crap. I wanted the same kinds of endorsements he had. My agent wasn't doing it for me, so I fired him.

"Jeremy came and spoke to me personally. He told me three days ago that he was going to make it happen, and he wanted me wearing Victory shoes before Wimbledon. So last night, I asked him about it. I wanted to know what the holdup was."

"What did he tell you?"

"That the lawyers always have their hands in this stuff, and it always takes longer than he wants it to. He was very apologetic. He told me I was welcome to come by and see him today, and he'd talk me through everything, but that it was going to take another few weeks to get all the details ironed out."

"And how did you react to that revelation?" Violet asked.

El simply shrugged. "It is what it is, you know? I thought it would have been done, and I admit, I lost my temper. I was angry, because I wanted that endorsement money. I crossed a line. But Jeremy was good about it. He understood my frustration, and I left the conversation feeling, well, perhaps not perfectly all right, but I was satisfied."

"Wait, what do you mean, you crossed a line?" I asked. "We saw the video footage. It's not like you punched him."

"No. But I confronted Jeremy in public. I used heated words, and I raised my voice. That's not the kind of person I strive to be. I was embarrassed about my actions afterwards."

I raised my eyebrows. This guy couldn't have been more different from Kristof. I could see what Sid meant about him being rather ordinary.

"Did you have any reason to want Jeremy Flagstaff dead?" Violet asked.

El's eyes widened incredulously. "What? Me? No, of course not. Not in a million years. I'd never kill anyone. And why would I kill Jeremy?"

"Did you know that he was going to renege on your deal? The reason it wasn't done yet was that he wasn't going to go through with it," Violet said, leaning forward.

El looked confused. "No, that's not right. Jeremy was very enthusiastic about it. He always said so."

"And Sid?"

"Yeah. Yeah, him too," El said. "Both of them. They told me the deal was going ahead, every time. I had no reason not to believe them. Why wouldn't I? Everyone knows how much the deal with Kristof was worth. I'd probably be getting a similar amount. Sure, I was impatient, but Jeremy told me I was going to get my deal. I'd be getting my money. It wasn't a problem."

"Can you think of anyone who might have wanted Jeremy dead?"

"Well, Kristof certainly wasn't pleased with him. But would he actually kill the man? I don't know. I'd like to think not. I play him regularly, and I'd rather not believe that someone I see at least once every few months is a cold-blooded killer. But what do I know? Perhaps that's wishful thinking on my part."

"What about other than Kristof?" I asked. "Is there anyone else you can think of?"

"No. But I know virtually nothing about Jeremy's life. We weren't friends. Although, that said, you should look at Sid."

"Oh?" I asked.

"I mean, okay, maybe he had nothing to do with it. But I heard the two of them arguing last night, in the men's room. About an hour before Jeremy was killed."

"What did you hear?" Violet asked, her eyes gleaming.

"Uh, I'm not entirely sure. I don't know what it means, at least. I was in one of the stalls, just taking a bit of a break. There were a lot of people there, you know? So I was just playing on my phone when the two of them walked in. Sid told Jeremy that he had to stop. I don't know what they were talking about. Jeremy then told Sid they were going to talk about it another time; he didn't want to do it here. Sid told Jeremy that he was tired of being treated like he didn't have a say and that there was a reason the two of them had gone into business as partners, and that Jeremy wasn't more important than he was. Jeremy then told Sid not to burn a bridge right here and now. He understood Sid's position, but he wanted the two of them to discuss it later. Sid told Jeremy he was just trying to get his own way and that he wasn't going to get away with this. He'd be sorry. Then Jeremy left."

"And you have no idea what they were talking about?" Violet asked.

El shook his head. "Sorry. Not a clue. Wish I could help."

"Do you know Sid as well?"

"About the same as I know Jeremy. If I saw him on the street, I'd say hi to him, but it's not like I've been to his house for dinner or anything like that. I've just seen him at events here and there."

"What is the impression you have of him?"

El paused for a moment. "Ruthless. I think he's a ruthless man who would stop at nothing to get what he wants, to the detriment of everybody around him. Do I think he could have killed Jeremy? Yes, I do. I read somewhere once that something like one percent of the population are psychopaths but that the majority of them don't grow up to be serial killers. You find them in boardrooms, instead. That's exactly the impression I got from Sid."

"All right, thank you," Violet said, standing and holding out a hand, which El shook. "We appreciate the help."

"Of course. Sorry I couldn't be of more use, but as I said, I didn't really know the man all that well. If there's anything else you need from me though, don't hesitate. You've got my number, haven't you?"

"Yes," Violet replied. "Thank you."

"I have one question," I said with a smile. "What do you think of your nickname? Racketman?"

El rolled his eyes. "I wish my parents had named me literally anything else, let's put it that way. But I suppose as far as nicknames go, it's not too bad, is it? There's certainly been worse. It's got a certain charm to it. Still, it'd be nice to be known for who I am as opposed to constantly being compared to one of the greatest musicians this country's ever known."

"I can understand that."

"But if that's the worst thing I've ever got to deal with in life, I'm not doing too badly, am I?" he offered up with a smile as we reached the front door.

We said goodbye and left, with Violet almost immediately pulling out her phone and tapping away on it. When she was done, she turned to me. "Do you have any impressions about him?"

I shrugged. "What was it that Sid said? He was the most boring person ever? Honestly, that's the impression that I got too. He didn't say anything remotely… I don't know, controversial? Not that I was really expecting him to. But he seemed to almost make an effort to not have a strong opinion about anything."

"Well, he was also trying to convince us he is not a murderer," Violet said with a smile.

"True," I admitted. "What are you looking up?"

"I want to speak with El's former agent. I think that would be interesting. We are not meeting with Kristof until later this afternoon, after his match, so we have the time. The agent, Simon Purcell, works in the City."

Chapter 6

Simon's office was all glass, white walls, and framed photos of athletes he represented. I'd never heard of him, but I had certainly heard of some of the athletes whose pictures were on his wall. Some of the biggest stars of the soccer, rugby, and tennis worlds were under Simon Purcell's banner.

When we arrived, Violet introduced herself as working with the police, which intimidated the receptionist enough into allowing us to see him immediately.

As soon as we entered, Simon stood up, opening his arms to us like we were old friends as he led us to comfortable, leather-backed chairs. "Come in, come in. How can I help the police with this investigation?" His accent was American. If I'd had to guess, I'd have said he was from New York. He just had that kind of attitude. Or maybe I'd just been in London too long.

Violet didn't correct him. "We are hoping you could tell us about Elton John, the athlete you used to represent."

Simon roared with laughter, and I took an immediate dislike to him. It was the kind of laugh that didn't sound fake but obviously was. He wore an expensive suit, his face was clean-shaven, and he had that kind of pseudo-casual air about him, like he wanted to be your best friend, but if you crossed him, he would slit your throat without a second thought. I suspected he was in his late forties, but it was hard to tell. Given the way his facial muscles didn't move quite right, I knew he got regular Botox injections, and I suspected he probably had more than that done in order to keep a youthful appearance.

"Oh, El. Yes, you're right, I used to be his agent." Simon leaned back in his chair and actually propped his feet up on his desk. "Don't tell me you think he could have done this? That's why you're here, of course. Jeremy Flagstaff and the party last night. Am I right?"

"Yes, that is correct."

"I was there, actually."

Violet raised an eyebrow. "You were not on the list of attendees that I received from the manager at the bar."

"Well, I had to duck out a little early. But you

can't think the hottest party in town was going down and I wouldn't have managed to snag an invite, can you? Of course I was there. I represent three of the athletes competing at Wimbledon this year, and this is the best opportunity to get their faces in front of the people who make the money decisions."

"Did you speak with Jeremy Flagstaff?" Violet asked.

"Sure did. Right at the beginning of the night. Wanted to know why he was letting go of my boy, Kristof."

"Wait, you also represent Kristof Mayer?" I asked.

Simon grinned at me. "He's one of my top earners. Nothing sells like a bad boy. I know he's got a bit of a reputation, but he's never crossed the line before. Well, okay, maybe he's snuck a toe over it now and again, but it's nothing that couldn't be fixed by just staying under the radar for a few weeks. But other than that, he's golden. I still don't understand why Victory Shoes dropped him."

"You don't know?" Violet asked.

"Not a clue. I think Kristof is hiding something from me though. I asked him about it, and he was cagey about his answer. I'll tell you one thing though: if I find out there was something hinky going on, the lawyers are getting involved. Do you know how much Kristof's deal was worth to me? Enough that I'm going to fight Jer and Sid on it.

Well, I guess just Sid now. But Jeremy didn't deserve this. He was a good man. A fair man."

"What about El?" Violet asked. "What did you think of him? We were told he fired you."

"Oh, is that what he's telling people? Nah. That whiny son-of-a wasn't making me enough money, so I dropped him. Told him I was getting too busy, couldn't organize deals for him anymore. He was angry about it too. First time I'd ever seen him get mad. It's too bad, you know? If he'd shown a bit more spunk over the years, maybe I would have been able to convince people to sign him for more money. But the guy was just a piece of white bread slathered with mayonnaise. Literally the plainest thing you can imagine. Nobody wants a guy that fades into the background on their campaign posters. And it's too bad too. I mean, he has the best name in sports, doesn't he? Elton John. Nicknamed Racketman. There's so much you can do with that. But he just had to be the most boring man alive. What a shame. An absolute shame."

"So you were the one who fired him. When was this?"

"Four months ago. I was streamlining my business. And sure, he had some deals. He was bringing in some money. I mean, the guy is a top-ranked tennis player. He's not some scrub getting into the tournaments through the lottery. But he doesn't bring in the same kind of money as the bigger personalities. And I mean, look at me. I'm a big personality. I have this office, I drive a Bugatti, I'm all about big, baby. So if an athlete doesn't deliver, he's got to go. And that was the case with El. But I don't hold a grudge against him or anything. He's a nice guy. Nicer than most, actually. Very polite. Soft-spoken. But he doesn't sell. That's just business. Nothing against the guy."

"Do you think he could have killed Jeremy?" I asked.

Simon snorted. "Are you kidding? Of course not. No, you're way off base there. El is the perfect Englishman. He probably would have just written a letter to his MP, which he would have described as 'heated' because he used the word 'damn' in it at one point."

"Did you know that El was in talks with Jeremy to represent Victory Shoes after Kristof was fired?" Violet asked.

Simon's feet dropped from his desk almost as quickly as his mouth fell open, and he leaned forward, staring at Violet. "No way."

She tilted her head slightly. "Yes. We have confirmed it."

"Are you kidding me? They dropped Kristof, and they're going to pick up El? Not a chance. Sid wouldn't allow it. Jeremy, I can see him thinking it's a good idea. But Sid is too smart for that."

"It is true, the two of them argued about it," Violet said. "What about Sid? Do you know him well?"

"Sure. Well enough. He's the real brains behind Flagstaff Group, as much as Jeremy presents himself as the face of it. He knows what he's doing when it comes to business. One of the smartest men I've ever come across. And completely ruthless. The kind of man who would slice his own mother's head off if someone offered him enough money for it."

"Ah. In that case, you believe he would kill Jeremy Flagstaff?"

"Sure, if he thought it would be worth it for him. But why would it be? Jeremy is the public front of the whole company. Sid knows that he's more of a behind-the-scenes man. He's smart enough to realize he doesn't have Jeremy's charisma, and he needs someone like that out there shaking hands and making friends with everyone while he sits in the background and schemes and works out the nitty-gritty details of every deal. The two of them are a package. They don't work without the other. That said, if Sid thought it was advantageous to him to get rid of Jeremy, I don't doubt for a second that he would do it. Do not let your guard down around that man. He spots your weaknesses, and he will take advantage of them."

"Good to know," I said with a smile.

"Who do you think killed Jeremy?" Violet asked.

Simon shrugged. "Above my pay grade, sorry. Wouldn't have a clue. All I can tell you is it wasn't me. I was long gone by the time it all went down."

"And how did the night go for you?" I asked. "Did you meet any potential new clients?"

"Sure did. I ran into that young woman from Canada, Emily Connors. Now her, she's golden right now. And did you know she hasn't even got an agent yet? She didn't think she needed one. I spoke to her for about five minutes, but she seemed rather freaked out about the whole thing. Eventually ran off. That's all right. I'll speak with her again at the tournament, let her know that I have her best interests at heart. I can make that girl a lot of money, and for years to come. She's only eighteen, which means she has one heck of a career ahead of her. She'll be set for life when she retires from tennis—I can make sure of that. Anyway, I chatted with her for a bit, and then I got a call a little later and left. Unrelated to any of this; my daughter broke her leg playing rugby, and I obviously had to go to the hospital."

"Sorry to hear."

"Thank you. She's all right. She's a trooper, my Melanie. She's hoping to make the Rugby 7s squad and play at the next Olympics. She'll probably make it too." Simon beamed with pride at the mention of his daughter. "She's great. And it could have been worse. Simple break has her out eight weeks. An ACL would have been months. All in all, she's okay. But it means I was gone before anything happened with Jeremy. I saw him as I was leaving, and he was speaking with someone. But Jeremy was always in somebody's ear. It was how he lived."

"All right, thank you for your time," Violet said.

"Of course." Simon stood up and shook our hands, and the two of us left.

Violet checked her watch as we went back down to ground level. "What do you say we visit your boyfriend? He should have done something with the body by now."

Chapter 7

We reached the morgue and found the two DCIs already in there.

DCI Fletcher scowled as soon as he spotted us. "What are you doing here? This is my case."

"And I have decided that I will also be investigating," Violet replied. "If you have a problem with that, I recommend you take it up with Superintendent Williams."

The former DCI Williams had been promoted, in large part because he was more than happy to accept Violet's expertise whenever she decided to join in on cases that happened to fall within his purview. Given the high-profile nature of this particular case, I knew that wasn't going to be a problem.

"Look, you know what? It doesn't matter. We already know who did it. We're just looking for the proof now."

"Oh, you do, do you?" Violet asked with a smile.

"And who might that be?"

"I'm not going to tell *you*," DCI Fletcher said.

"If your goal was to do a great impression of a seven-year-old on the playground, you absolutely nailed it," I told the police officer, giving him two thumbs up.

He grimaced. "Why are you even here? You aren't a detective at all. You're just her little puppy that trails along after her."

"Ah, Doctor Coburn," Jake said suddenly, emerging from one of the doors, holding a file in his hand. "It's good to see you. And you, Violet."

"Jake," she replied in greeting while I looked smugly over at DCI Fletcher. I wasn't the kind of person who insisted on being referred to by my title by anyone and everyone, but it certainly did stop DCI Fletcher in his tracks, which was why Jake had used it. I didn't think he'd ever called me that before in his life.

"So, I did the autopsy on Jeremy Flagstaff this morning. It's going to take a few days for toxicology to come back with an official report, but unofficially, you're looking at cyanide," Jake said, flipping through the pages.

"Wait, you can't say any of this in front of *her*," DCI Fletcher snapped, looking at Violet.

"Seeing as I am the one who told you cyanide was the cause of death, it is not as though I have gleaned any special insights from that one sentence," Violet said, deadpan. "Now, we both know that I will be getting this information. The question is whether you will continue to hold up this investigation, or if you will simply accept that I have decided to investigate alongside you. After all, do we not both benefit if the killer is found? Yes, of course we do. It does not matter who finds him."

"She has a point," DCI Johnson said to his superior.

"No one asked you," Fletcher scowled back, but then he turned to Jake. "All right, let's have it."

"Frankly, there isn't much here. Jeremy Flagstaff's liver wasn't in great shape, but it would have been too early for him to notice any symptoms, and given the condition of his blood vessels, I suspect he had high blood pressure. He would have been taking medication for it, which the toxicology report will reveal, but other than that, I'm afraid I don't have much that will help."

"His death was nearly instant, is that correct?" Violet asked.

Jake nodded. "Yes. Within a minute or two would be my guess."

"That lines up with what we saw at the time," Violet replied with a nod.

"So you don't have anything else to help us prove who the killer is?" DCI Fletcher said. "Great. I guess we'll have to go out and get it on our own."

"Yes, heaven forbid you actually go out and do policework," Violet replied.

DCI Fletcher glared at her and motioned for

DCI Johnson to follow him, and he went off. DCI Johnson shot the two of us an apologetic glance before trailing his partner.

When they left, Jake shot the two of us a shrug. "Sorry I can't hand you the killer on a silver platter. There wasn't all that much to get from this body that would help you solve the case."

"It is all right," Violet said with a smile. "This case, it is turning out to be much more interesting than I had initially expected it to be."

"Does that mean you know who did it?" I asked.

"I am certainly beginning to form an opinion as to how the crime was committed and why. However, knowing what was done and being able to prove it are two very different things. And besides, it is still very early in the investigation. Who is to say that what I have decided is correct? I am certain there is plenty of information out there still to be gathered, which may change my perception of the facts as I see them now."

"That was the most convoluted 'no' I've ever heard," Jake said to Violet with a grin.

"Well, you know me. When I know for certain who did it and why, I will let everyone know."

"How was the party otherwise?"

"I mean, a guy dropping dead in the middle is always a bit of a buzzkill," I replied.

"Okay, I guess I walked into that one. Still. Did you get to meet anyone interesting?"

"Yeah, Emily Connors. Although technically

she's a suspect too. She would have had the opportunity to slip the cyanide into Jeremy's drink, though I don't think she did. She doesn't have a motive. At least, not that we know of."

"What was she like?"

"Shy. A bit nervous. Frankly, I don't blame her one bit. She's young, and she's suddenly found herself playing against some of the people she's looked up to her entire life. Everything has kind of exploded for her, in a good way. And I can relate to that, although a bit differently. I think sometimes, your life can change completely in an instant, and it takes some time for your head to wrap itself around that idea."

"For sure. That's great though."

"I actually spent most of the night talking to her. I saw a bunch of other people though. I also met Jeremy Flagstaff, only briefly, before he died."

"Did you happen to have any cyanide on you?"

"Ha ha," I deadpanned. "You're so funny."

"Thank you, I think so. I've heard he's very charming in real life. Was."

"Yeah, definitely. Simon, the players' agent we spoke to, who gets endorsement deals for his athletes, he said that Sid is the real brains behind the whole operation though. And having met the guy, I can see it. He's obviously smart. Shrewd, I should say. He doesn't have the same sparkling personality that Jeremy did, but I can understand why they worked well together."

"Teamwork makes the dream work."

"Certainly true in their case. Although I'm wondering if the dream had stopped working. It sounds like the two of them weren't getting along. They were arguing over endorsement deals."

"That sounds like a promising motive for murder," Jake said, raising an eyebrow.

"It is," Violet replied. "And in fact, the more I learn about this case, the more I am certain that it centers around this argument regarding the endorsement deal."

"Yeah, that's what everything keeps coming back to. And one of our other suspects, Kristof, was mad at Jeremy for having torn up his contract. He just lost millions of pounds overnight. I mean, I know he's not in the bread line or anything, but that still has to hurt."

"Of course, that's the guy who was in the news a few months ago," Jake said. "He's the one who threw a ball at the poor ball boy when he thought he did a bad job, right? And then pretended it was an accident so he wouldn't get disqualified?"

"That's the one."

Jake shook his head. "That just shouldn't be allowed. I mean, I get it. The stakes are high, and there's pressure. But they're kids. That job has to be a highlight of their life. And they do it so well, especially since some of them are so young. How can you possibly get so angry at a kid that you throw a ball at them? Come on. If you ask me, he should have been disqualified from the tournament on the spot."

"I agree," I said. "But he's so good, he gets away with anything."

"Yeah. And that's part of the problem. Not just in tennis but in sports in general. Luckily, attitudes seem to be changing. There are more discussions around mental health and making sure that athletes have an appropriate work environment, like everyone else who goes to work every day, even if they're not the best in the world at what they do. Of course, even someone as good at tennis as Kristof Mayer isn't going to get away with it if he committed murder. Not with you two on the case."

I returned Jake's grin. "Well, we'll see. I admit, I instinctively thought it was him, but the psychology isn't right. Whoever did this planned it ahead of time. They had to get access to the cyanide, for one thing. Which, admittedly, isn't hard these days thanks to the dark web. But it still required planning."

"Yes. Whoever did this thought it through. They knew what they were going to do," Violet said. "It was no accident. But I will solve this crime in the end. I do not know if the killer was aware of my presence, but I cannot let it stand, regardless."

"Violet is taking it as a personal affront that someone thought they could murder another human being with her in the same room," I explained to Jake.

"Ah. I was wondering what she saw in this case that was so interesting."

"It's a puzzle, for sure. Actually, it's more like a Gordian knot. Everything is tangled together, and it's about pulling all the strands apart."

"Or you could just do what Alexander the Great did and slice through the whole thing with a sword," Jake said with a wink.

"Right now, that doesn't sound like the worst idea. But we'll see. We're going to go see Kristof. He should be playing his first match today."

"Well, good luck. I hope you find your killer and get them safely under lock and key."

"Thanks."

"Sorry I couldn't be more help," Jake said with a shrug. "Sometimes the bodies have a story to tell, and sometimes they don't. Jeremy's told a story of a life well lived, but it didn't have many clues to reveal about his death. Feel free to text if you have any questions though."

"We will," I promised.

Violet and I left the morgue.

"That wasn't especially useful," I grumbled. "I was hoping the body would have more to tell us."

"A lack of information is still information," Violet replied. "It appears that it is not helpful to us now, but who knows? It is still early, and we have not spoken to the man who has a better motive than anyone else so far."

"True. Still, I can ask for a lot. Like a little ghost

that pops out of the body when Jake cuts it open and says in a high-pitched voice, 'Sid killed me! It was him!'"

Violet laughed. "The world would be a lot less interesting if every solution was handed to you by a small ghost."

"I mean, in a way. It would also be a lot *more* interesting in other ways."

"That is true," Violet admitted.

"Excuse me," a voice said behind us.

I turned to see DCI Johnson following us.

"Yes, DCI?" Violet said.

"Look, I know DCI Fletcher is short with you, but I know your reputation. I know how good you are. You should know: we received an anonymous tip letting us know that Sid Miller bought cyanide and that it was in his office. We searched it—he allowed us to—and didn't find any though."

"Thank you very much for the information," Violet said. "Do you know who left the tip, unoffically?"

DCI Johnson shook his head. "It was anonymous. Whoever left the message used one of those apps that disguises your voice."

Although Violet very much enjoyed a challenge, I would have been very happy with a tiny ghost telling me who the killer was. But since that wasn't an option, I was going to have to help figure it out the hard way. And that meant interviewing one of the athletes with the worst temper imaginable.

Chapter 8

The exterior of the All England Lawn Tennis and Croquet Club, the location of Wimbledon, with an appropriately long name, was stunning. Of course, having watched tennis on TV, I knew what the inner courts looked like. But the exterior was impressive. Glass jutted from the building, whose ivy-covered walls did a great job of hiding its growing age.

Violet and I had our IDs ready and were quickly waved through into the Center Court building.

I didn't know who she'd contacted, but someone knew we were coming, and a sharply dressed security guard led us through the halls and to the men's locker room.

"Just a moment, will you? I'll make sure he's ready for you," the security guard said before stepping into the room. He emerged a moment later. "You can go in."

I smiled my thanks as I passed him and entered the men's locker room. It was the end of the day now, and all the tennis had been played. The room had cleared out except for Kristof Mayer, who sat on one of the honey-colored wooden benches.

The locker room was a little bit dated, as if it was a relic on the verge of having aged so much it would be considered retro. Still, it was in good shape. The gray-blue, lightly patterned carpet underfoot was clean, and wooden benches sat in rows, with a number of lockers available for players to use at the end of the room. Fluorescent light bathed the room in a cool glow.

Kristof Mayer's hair was still damp from his shower, and he looked up at us with a cool gaze. He was dressed in slacks and a polo, a bag with the Victory Shoes logo at his feet. I suppose they hadn't gone public with the contract termination just yet.

"You are the famous detective," he said to Violet, only the slightest hint of an Austrian accent in his voice. "The one who asked to speak to me."

"Yes," she replied. "And this is my co-worker, Cassie Coburn."

Kristof eyed me with cool detachment as if trying to work out what I was all about. Well, two could play at that game. I maintained eye contact with him, neither one of us blinking, until finally, he turned away.

"What is it that you want to know?"

"Did you kill Jeremy Flagstaff?"

"I wish I had," Kristof replied. "He was awful. Just the worst man. I'm not sorry he's dead, and think of me what you will for that opinion. There are plenty of other people in this world I'll save my pity for. But I'm not the one who killed him. He wouldn't be worth the risk of a prison stay."

I raised my eyebrows. This was certainly one way of addressing the issue. Admit you hate the guy but that you didn't kill him. I wasn't sure it made him look less guilty though.

"Good, so there is no need to beat around the bush," Violet said. "Jeremy was going to kill your endorsement deal and invoke the morals clause because you thought it was acceptable to commit assault at a club in Berlin, and it got out."

"Yes, and it is total bull. I did it, I admit that. But I only admit it because you already know. I paid everyone off. That woman, her life is so much better with a million more euros than it was without it. She did not suffer from the event overall. It was all blown out of proportion."

"You cannot be serious," I interrupted. "Are you actually trying to argue that the woman is now better off because you punched her in the face?"

Kristof shrugged. "The way I see it, she is. It was a moment of discomfort for her, and now she has a sizeable amount of cash to use for the rest of her life."

I pressed my fingers against the bridge of my nose and forced myself to take a couple deep breaths. But because I wasn't a spontaneous tennis player with literally zero self-control, I decided not to grab the fire extinguisher off the wall and smash him in the face with it.

I was tempted though.

"If only you had asked the woman her preference *before* you decided to make the decision for her," Violet said calmly. "Then she would actually have had a say in the whole incident. But it is done. And it has cost you your biggest sponsorship."

"I don't know how they even found out about it. If I ever do discover who ratted me out, I will sue them into next year. It was supposed to be hushed up. No one was supposed to know it happened. Everyone makes mistakes. But Jeremy, oh no, Jeremy had to pretend that he was Mister Perfect all the time. He knew what he was getting into with me. He knew that my attitude and my reputation are what sell the shoes. Otherwise, he would go after that bland Englishman with the silly name, like the singer. You want someone boring who will never make a mistake? That is him. You want someone with passion, who understands that's what makes people talk about you. Being in the news all the time, that's me."

"Yes, that worked out absolutely brilliantly for you," I said dryly.

Kristof narrowed his eyes in my direction. "Look, I already said I made a mistake. It happens. I have a temper. Everybody knows that. But it's also what makes me such a good tennis player. When I get into that zone, nobody can stop me. Nobody."

"So prove to us that you did not get into that zone with Jeremy last night," Violet said, crossing her arms in front of her. "Because right now, all I see is an angry brute of a man attempting to excuse his behavior and who has given me exactly zero reason to believe he is innocent of the crime of which he is a suspect."

A low growl emerged from the back of Kristof's throat. "Do you really think I would kill the bastard over that deal? No, of course not. I was mad at him. I admit that. And I showed up that night and confronted him. I wanted Jeremy to know that I wasn't pleased. I wanted him to be afraid of me. I admit that. But I didn't kill him. I wouldn't kill him. And you can't prove I did it."

Kristof raised his chin in Violet's direction as if daring her to prove otherwise. I hated this guy. Everything about him made me want to punch him in the mouth. But of course, because I had better willpower than he did, I didn't.

"We will see," Violet replied.

"Let me guess, you think that's a threat," Kristof mocked. "Well, guess what. You can't do anything to me. I didn't kill Jeremy. Yeah, I argued with him. I was pissed. You would be too if someone was going to tear up your seventy-two-million-pound contract because you made a little mistake, and you fixed it. No one was going to find out about the incident in Berlin. I took care of it. And let me tell you this too: if you go to the media about this, or if I find out that this incident makes the news, I will be sending my lawyers after you. I do not know how you found out about it, but you don't tell anyone. Understood?"

Violet stood up, her eyes flashing. "You think that's a threat? Because let me explain something to you. I do not care that you are more skilled at hitting a ball into a small square than most other people in the world. It does not interest me in the least. You believe yourself to be invincible because no one ever holds you to account for anything that you do. But how would you like it if the world found out that you replaced your competition's shoes with weighted ones at Indian Wells last year? Do you think that would go well for you?"

Kristof was, for probably the first time in his life, left speechless. His mouth opened and closed, and he finally stammered out, "Wh... what?"

"Oh, all of a sudden *Monsieur Attitude* does not have anything to say?" Violet provoked.

"How do you know about that? *Nobody* knows about that."

"That is because nobody pays attention."

"It was fifty grams!"

"And it made a difference. No one else saw it, but I did. Oh, but if that came out, it would be so much worse than even committing an assault. Your entire career would be over. And then where does that leave you? So again, I say, do not threaten me. Because I always know more than you know."

I had to hide my own shock as best I could. Kristof was a cheater? At tennis? Wow. That was certainly something. And yet here he was, basically admitting it. Violet hadn't said a thing before. I wondered why not.

Kristof narrowed his eyes at Violet. "You still can't prove it."

"Is that really a risk you want to take?" Violet replied, a small smile appearing at the corner of her mouth.

"Fine. What will it take for you to not tell anyone about what happened in Berlin?"

"You answer all of my questions honestly. And believe me, I will know if you are lying. I know that you sabotaged the shoes. I can easily tell if you are not telling me the truth."

I could practically see the fight leaving Kristof Mayer's eyes. He was a defeated man, and he knew it. "All right. Fine." His voice was surly, like that of a child who had just been caught with his hand in the cookie jar and was now being punished.

"Do you know Emily Connors?"

"The new kid who's been winning on the women's circuit? I met her once. She is shy, reserved. I got the impression she was afraid of me. She appears harmless."

"Do you know of any reason she might have had to kill Jeremy?"

Kristof snorted. "No, of course not."

"What about Sid, his business partner? What do you think of him?"

Mayer pursed his lips. "He does his best to pull the strings behind the curtain. But it does not always work. I have heard that Sid did not want to cancel my deal. He wanted to be more prudent than Jeremy, and he wanted to see how it all played out. Smart man. As I said, I plugged all of the holes. So no, I had nothing against Sid."

"Which means that with Jeremy out of the way, you have a better chance at keeping your contract," I pointed out.

"I do not know for certain. That is for lawyers and agents who know how all of that stuff works to figure out. All I know is that I was told the contract was over. I assumed that was it. What good would it have done to kill Jeremy after the fact? I do not expect things to be different. Do I feel as though I was ripped off? Yes. Of course. But do I think I could do anything to change it? No. I have told you, I did not kill Jeremy."

"Who do you think did?" Violet asked.

"I think it was Sid. He and Jeremy did not appear to be getting along, and I do not trust the man. He is... what they call in English slimy. Very slimy. He is out for himself and only himself."

That was certainly interesting. Kristof was now the second person we'd spoken to today who thought Sid might be the killer.

"Do you have any proof it might have been him?"

Kristof scowled. "What do you want, for me to do your entire job for you? No, I do not. It is not as though the two of us are best friends."

"Well, if he wanted to save your sponsorship deal, maybe you should have been," I offered.

"What would you know about anything?" Kristof snapped in my direction. "I do not even know why you are here."

"I'm the muscle behind the operation," I deadpanned.

"Focus, Kristof," Violet said. "What else do you have for us?"

"Nothing. I don't know anything else. I told you, I didn't kill Jeremy. I don't know who did. Deal with it."

"All right. If it is as you say, we will leave."

"Good," Kristof growled. "I never want to see either of you again."

I turned to go, figuring the conversation was over. Violet was behind me, and a second later, I heard a little bit of a scuffle.

Kristof had risen from his seat and stepped quickly toward Violet. He was going to attack her.

Before I got the chance to call out to her, however, Violet turned. With a quick movement, she swept underneath Kristof's reach and shoved him against the wall, pressing her entire body against his.

Kristof's arm was twisted behind him, and he shouted, "What the hell are you doing?"

"I could snap your arm like a twig if I wanted to right now," Violet said quietly into his ear, just loudly enough for me to hear. "I could ruin your tournament and your life. Is that what you want? Because I do not like bullies, and that is what you are. A bully."

"You wouldn't dare," Kristof replied, and a moment later, he let out a small squeal. "All right. All right. I'll leave you alone. I promise."

Violet stepped backward while I kept a very close eye on the fire extinguisher in case we needed to use it as a weapon. But Kristof stepped backward, clutching his right arm, his eyes aflame. He was angry. Extremely angry. He obviously had zero self-control.

I left the room, and Violet followed. Neither one of us spoke until we were back on the train, speeding back toward central London.

Chapter 9

"Well," Violet finally said about ten minutes into our journey.

I was used to her process. She liked to think after interviews, so I never interrupted her until she was ready to speak.

"That was certainly an adventure."

"It makes me wonder how many other 'mistakes' Kristof made that he just paid off," I said dryly, using air quotes.

"Indeed. I would suspect that it has happened more than once. I suspect that if one person came forward, the entire house of cards would tumble. Kristof is obviously aware. His actions with us, the threats, they are meant to warn us away from revealing what kind of man he is."

"How did you know he cheated at the tournament last year?" I asked.

Violet smiled. "When it was revealed that

Kristof was one of the suspects, I went back and watched some of his games from the past year. I noticed something at the Indian Wells tournament, and it was that Kristof appeared quicker on his feet than all of his competitors. It was barely noticeable, of course, but my entire career has been built around noticing things others do not. I then went and watched the other games of his competitors, and I came to the conclusion that Kristof likely tampered with their equipment. Most likely their shoes. Of course, for someone like you and me, adding a few grams of weight to a pair of shoes would be completely unnoticeable. But for athletes at that level, where a tenth of a second or a few centimeters of distance is the difference between being able to return a serve and not, it is of vital importance."

"Right. So he would have slipped something weighted into the shoes, something subtle enough that it wouldn't have been noticed."

"*Exactement.* The athletes likely would have noticed that they felt a bit sluggish but chalked it up to their own routines. I do not believe they would have thought their competitor would have sabotaged them. Or perhaps they did, and Kristof was able to remove the weight before they noticed. I do not know the details, but I know that he did it."

"He should be kicked off the tour," I said darkly.

"Yes. But alas, there is no evidence. As much as I

believe my word should be considered proof, it is not so. I was able to use my knowledge to surprise and destabilize Kristof in conversation, but that is all. Still, it worked. And we were able to see exactly what kind of man he is. A brute. A bully. As we thought, someone with no ability to control his own emotions. The question is, has he already dug himself too big a hole? Is he the killer? He certainly is a man who belongs in prison. But proving it is a whole other matter."

"I hope he did it. You're right, he does belong in jail. He's an abuser. He even tried to strong-arm you."

"Yes. Luckily, while he was busy learning to play tennis, I was studying judo. Being skilled in the arts of self-defense is prudent in my line of work. But it was interesting, did you not think? He has a very strange psychology, Kristof. It is as though he is incapable of knowing when to stop. Everything with him is aggression, aggression, aggression."

"It was hard not to notice that," I said dryly. "Do you think he killed Jeremy though? I don't know, personally. It's hard. He certainly had motive, but even he admits it. And he didn't give us any reason he didn't do it, but of course, it's hard to prove a negative. You can't entirely hold that against him."

"No. I must think. I have my little idea, but I do not know yet if it is true. And if it is, I do not know how I will prove it to be. I have to think."

"Wait, you have an idea? Is it Sid? Or Kristof?"

"I do not want to say at the moment, as I am not certain that I am right."

I was used to Violet being like that. Frankly, I didn't really have a clue who had done it. As much as I hated to admit it, I didn't think Kristof was the killer. I figured if he had done it, he would have just attacked Jeremy on the spot. He didn't seem to me to be the kind of person who could plan a crime, let alone someone who could plan a crime *and* get away with it for more than five minutes with Violet Despuis in the room.

No, it had to be someone else. But who? There was always El. But I didn't like his motive. He had been upset with Jeremy, yes, but ultimately, there was a deal to be made with him. Jeremy had wanted El to be signed to the shoe company. It was Sid who didn't. So why would El kill Jeremy and not Sid if he was angry over the deal? It made zero sense.

"What is it that you think?" Violet asked me.

I told her what I'd just thought about.

"You are on the right track, I believe. This case, it is all about motive. Everyone has the opportunity. Any of the people we have spoken to, and Emily Connors, *could* have poisoned the champagne. Any of them could have gone onto the dark web and ordered cyanide. It is not that difficult these days, thanks to the internet, to access it. That leaves us with motive. And that is the puzzle we deal with."

"Yeah, but more than one person has a motive in this case."

"That is the puzzle. We have to navigate it and follow the threads. In this instance, I believe it is slightly more complex than it appears at first glance."

I knew Violet wasn't going to give me any more than that when it came to telling me what she was thinking, so I just settled in for the rest of the train ride and thought about the case as we sped back toward downtown London.

WHEN WE GOT BACK HOME, MY STOMACH WAS grumbling, and I was pleased to enter the apartment to find Jake at the kitchen counter, chopping up vegetables as he made spaghetti sauce.

"Yum, that smells delicious. I haven't eaten anything all day."

"Wow, you must really be struggling then," Jake teased. "Normally, you can't go more than an hour without food. It must be a big case."

I shoved him teasingly, grabbing some slices of bell pepper as I did so and munching away.

"So, how did the case go? Solve it yet?" Jake asked.

"Nope. But I did meet one of the worst human beings I've ever had the displeasure of having a conversation with. Just in case you were wondering:

Kristof lives up to his reputation. And then some. He actually tried to attack Violet today."

Jake's eyes widened. "No kidding. I assume it went badly for him?"

I nodded. "Yup."

"One of the first cases I ever worked with Violet, she confronted one of the detectives investigating the case in my morgue. It turned out he was the killer. Complicated thing. Anyway, he decided to try and fight his way out. It ended badly for him as well. I've never worried about Violet in a fight since. She fights like she thinks. It's intelligent, and every move is calculated. She doesn't need brute strength; she gets away with thinking her way through it."

"Yeah, that appears to be what happened here. She managed to get Kristof against the wall, and she threatened to break his arm if he didn't leave us alone."

"Sounds about right. I'm glad you're okay."

"He's unbelievable. So, we mentioned the assault he committed on that woman in Berlin. He told us that she was better off having been hurt for a few minutes and getting a million-euro check than not. That's the kind of man he is."

Jake let out a low whistle. "He sounds like trouble."

"He is. There's a whole bunch to unpack here. And the worst part is, I'm not sure he's the killer. I mean, he could be. But ugh. This whole case is something else. Violet thought it was going to be super easy, but it's turning out to be more complex than she thought."

"The simplest-looking ones often do. That's the sign of a smart murderer, isn't it? It has to be simple. It's when things get super complicated that people get caught."

"You're right. And this one is simple. One of the people who went up to Jeremy Flagstaff poisoned his drink. The question is: why? And which one of them did it? It feels like it's hopeless."

"It's not hopeless. You and Violet will figure it out."

"Thanks for including me in that sentence," I said with a smile.

"Hey, if you weren't of any use to her, she wouldn't have you around. You might not think you're being all that useful when you hang around with her, but you are."

"I know," I said. "Though usually, there's a bit more science stuff that I get to lend my expertise to. But that's the case. It's weird. It feels like there's something I'm missing, and I don't like feeling this way."

"I'm sure you'll figure it out eventually though. Hopefully, no more bodies will show up. The police aren't going to get there. I've worked with DCI Fletcher before. He's got the IQ of a crayon. The other guy seems promising though."

"DCI Johnson? Yeah, I agree. He was talking to Violet at the crime scene, and Fletcher wasn't pleased about it. But he seemed to actually care about the psychology of a case, and that's important."

"Good."

"So we'll see. Maybe Violet is going to find herself a new DCI that she can actually work with regularly now that Williams has been promoted," I said with a smile.

"Here's hoping. That would be good for her."

I tried helping Jake with dinner, but he shooed me away and instead poured me a glass of merlot, which I sipped while giving him a longer version of the day's events. When dinner was finally ready, we settled down and watched a bit of TV—England has so many comedy quiz shows, I was starting to fall in love with them—then Sequoia began begging for a walk.

"I'll take her out," I said to Jake. "I'll be back in about twenty minutes."

"Sounds good."

As soon as I grabbed her leash, Sequoia knew what was happening and sprinted to the door, happily hopping up and down in excitement, her tail wagging madly as her tongue flew around in anticipation.

I looked over at Biscuit, but he was curled up in a ball on the couch, dead to the world. I figured if I tried to wake him up to see if he wanted to come, I'd probably get bitten.

"Looks like it's just you and me then, kiddo," I said to Sequoia as I clipped her up.

The two of us went out and began our slow meander around the neighborhood. Downtown London apparently had so many little spots to sniff, that was much more interesting than getting any sort of real exercise.

Personally, I enjoyed the fresh night air. It was late, nearly ten o'clock now, and since it was right around the solstice, the days were long. The sun had set, but not all that long ago, and the heat of the day was slowly dissipating into a comfortable coolness.

I took deep breaths, letting the stress and thoughts of the day flow away while my dog roamed. We walked around for about half an hour; I let Sequoia decide where to go. She went straight to Kensington Gardens, as she always did, but unfortunately for her, it was too late to enter. I tried to tell her, but it wasn't as if she could understand me. Or if she did, she chose to believe I was lying.

When she saw the wrought-iron gates at the entrance were shut, she turned and continued wandering around, and the two of us walked rather aimlessly through the neighborhood. The only time I really held firm was when Sequoia wanted to go down dark alleys. Sorry, doggo. Not in London at night.

After about thirty minutes, we headed back home. I was walking down Eldon Road when I noticed something strange. There was a car parked at the end of the street, and as I walked by, I saw someone sitting in the driver's seat.

That was a little bit strange by itself. Who would be sitting alone in a car by themselves? But then, when I walked past, the driver seemed to turn away from me, as if they specifically didn't want me to see them.

Alarm bells immediately began going off in my head. Someone was staking out our street.

I decided to act as if I hadn't noticed anything. I kept walking then pulled out my phone.

"Hey, Sequoia, aren't you a good girl," I said in a happy voice, opening the photo app. "You're so pretty! What a good dog!"

I took a few pictures, making sure to get the car in the background. Thanks to the streetlights, combined with clear skies and a bit of a moon, it wasn't nearly as dark as its occupant would probably have wanted it to be, and I was able to get a decent picture that included the license plate.

"You're such a good dog," I sang as I led Sequoia back home. I took another couple pictures of her further down the street to look less suspicious and then took her inside. As soon as I did, I locked the door behind me.

"There's someone in a car at the end of the street," I said to Jake.

He immediately looked concerned. "Did you see who it was? Are they going after Violet?"

"I didn't see them, and I don't know. That's what I'm worried about though. I should text her."

I pulled out my phone and had a look at the photo first. Jake looked over my shoulder. "You can make out the person in the car. Who is it?"

I squinted at the screen as I used my fingers to zoom in on the face. When I saw who it was, I gasped.

"That's DCI Johnson," Jake said.

"Yeah. What's he doing here, staking out our street?"

"Do you want me to go out there and ask him?"

I shook my head. "No. I'd rather he not know we're onto him. That explains why he turned away when I walked past though. I would have recognized him. Okay, we have to let Violet know."

I sent my friend a text. *Just FYI, DCI Johnson is staking out our street. He's in a black Renault at the western end.*

Her reply came through a moment later. *Yes, he has been there for just over an hour. Thank you for letting me know.*

What are you going to do about it?

I am working on another case at the moment, so, nothing. So long as he does nothing. But I have eyes on him.

I chewed on my lip as I considered my options. I didn't like that DCI Johnson was stalking Violet. Because let's face it, he was totally here for Violet and not me.

But more importantly: why? This wasn't some

newbie who wanted to ask her a question and was sitting in his car, trying to build up the courage. If it was, he wouldn't have tried to hide from me.

"I'm going to see what he's up to," I announced to Jake.

"Are you sure?"

I nodded. "Yeah. I want to know what he's doing. What he's about. Violet is working on another case right now."

"Okay. How can I help?"

"I need a car, because when he leaves, I have to be able to follow him. Can I take yours?"

"Of course."

Jake's car was parked out front of our place basically all the time. It wasn't as if it got much use here in downtown London, but he liked to take it instead of the train if we were going out to the country for the weekend.

He tossed me the keys, and I caught them easily, biting my lip.

"Do you want me to come?" he asked.

"I was actually hoping you might be able to distract him for me for a minute so I can get into the car without him noticing me."

"Sure. Are you going to be okay?"

I nodded. "I don't plan on doing anything dumb. I just want to follow him, see where he goes."

"Got it. Okay, let's do it."

Chapter 10

Five minutes later, the two of us had made our plan and were ready to go. I was dressed in black, my hair mostly tucked under a baseball cap. I had the car keys in my pocket.

Jake was dressed like he was heading for a night out at the pub. The two of us left together, but when Jake actually went out onto the street, I stayed crouched in the entrance to our basement suite, waiting to hear Jake's voice.

It came drifting over to me a minute later.

"Is that… oh, hi, mate. DCI Johnson, was it? Emmett? Yeah, Jake here. Nice to see you again. I had no idea you lived in the neighborhood."

Perfect. As Jake struck up a conversation with my mark, I scurried down to his car as fast as I could. Luckily, he drove a ten-year-old Corolla that didn't have any of those fancy features like lights that turned on automatically when you got close to it. As soon as I reached the car, I went to the driver's side and got in.

We had decided the best way to go about things was to stake out DCI Johnson back. After all, he might notice if I drove the car past him. So I sat in the car and waited, grateful that this was happening in June and not January.

Luckily, it didn't take long for him to get on the move. I spotted Jake heading back to our suite. He didn't so much as glance at the car on his way back, which I was grateful for. About two, maybe three minutes later, I heard the rumble of an engine coming to life, and I ducked low in the car. Headlights filled the interior as a vehicle passed by. After it moved past me, I turned to check it out; the detective was leaving.

Jake seeing him parked on our street must have spooked him. Perfect.

I turned on the car and made a U-turn, pulling out onto the road and following the detective. I gripped the wheel hard as my heart pounded. I didn't know where he was going. Didn't know why he had been watching Violet's place. But there was no way I was letting him go without finding out.

I kept my distance, staying back as far as I could without losing him completely. Luckily, he was headed for Kensington Road, which was jam-packed with traffic at the best of times, making it much easier for me to stay on his tail without being noticed.

DCI Johnson headed east, eventually parking on a street a few blocks away from St. Paul's Cathedral. In the interest of not generating too much suspicion, I continued past him then made a U-turn two intersections later.

I drove past the spot to find the detective entering a busy pub, and I made a mental note of the name. Parking my car a block away, I walked back toward it, cursing the fact that I hadn't worn a better disguise.

The pub was very traditionally British, with an exterior painted a shade of red that would have looked horrendous in any other city. The windows were decorated with bright colors advertising that it was a family-owned business and listing their new menu offerings.

I didn't want to go inside for fear of being spotted, so I waited about three minutes and then walked casually past the window. I kept my hat on to hide my face at least somewhat and glanced inside to see what DCI Johnson was doing.

What I saw made my blood freeze.

He was seated at a table with a woman. I could see both their profiles, and as soon as I saw hers, I froze.

He was speaking with Violet's sister, Lily.

Lily was basically what Violet could have been if she was a horrible human being. As Violet put it, her sister was the mastermind behind much of the criminal activity in London, but she was always able to keep herself an arm's length away so that she was never actually convicted of any crimes.

The fact that DCI Johnson had been watching Violet's place and was now meeting with Lily gave me hives.

Besides, the woman was smart. If she spotted me, even with the disguise, I knew she'd recognize me. I immediately hightailed it out of there and went back to the car. Could she have seen me?

No. Given the angles involved, it was impossible. She would have to have turned her head, and she hadn't done so before I left. Lily had no idea. I was sure of that.

I drove back home with adrenaline coursing through my veins. I pulled the car into the same spot it had been in when I left and practically dove back into the suite. It wasn't until I saw Jake's concerned face that I realized I must have looked like a crazy person.

"What is it? What's wrong? Are you okay?"

"It's Lily," I said breathlessly. "DCI Johnson is meeting with Lily."

Jake started. "What? Are you serious? Why?"

"I don't know. I just figured I had to get out of there. But it means Lily has got people in the Metropolitan Police working for her. Which, I mean, I'm not surprised. Someone as powerful as her, she would have to have people on the inside. But now, with Johnson being on this case and watching Violet? That's not a coincidence."

"I agree. Lily must have sent him to keep an eye on her. Especially with him trying to get her attention."

"And here I thought there might have just finally been another detective who recognized the wisdom in playing on Violet's team instead of against her," I said dryly. "I should have known better. Williams really does seem to have been exceptional."

"Yeah. So now the question is: what are you going to do?"

"I don't know," I said slowly. "Violet doesn't seem concerned. She's working on another case. She seemed to already know about DCI Johnson, so maybe it's not as big a thing as I think. Still, I don't like this at all. I think it could end up being important."

"Important to this case or important to life in general?" Jake asked.

I frowned as I thought about the answer. "I'd imagine life in general. It's not that I can't see Lily getting involved in Jeremy Flagstaff's murder. Actually, that's exactly the sort of thing I *could* imagine her doing. He was a powerful guy, and it might have suited her to get him out of the way. But I don't know how DCI Johnson could have gotten himself specifically assigned to that case. If he was the senior partner, I could imagine him convincing a higher-up to let him in on it. But he's not; Fletcher is. So no. I think this is more about life in general. I think Johnson was working for Lily, happened to see

Violet at a crime scene, got to know her, and is now spying on her for Lily. But why? I have no idea."

"All of that makes a lot of sense," Jake said with a nod. "What are you going to do?"

"I want to know who DCI Johnson really is. Not that I think he's hiding his identity or anything, but I want to look into him. I need information. The more I know, the better. And I'm going to tell Violet tomorrow. I think she should know if she doesn't already. Given her reaction, I wouldn't be surprised if she's already aware."

"True, me either. But I think your plan is a good one."

"Yeah. Even if it's just for my own peace of mind. I don't like knowing that there's someone out there, working for Lily, spying on Violet. Which, I mean, okay. She's probably been spied on a lot by her sister. The more I think about it, the more I wonder if this has been going on for ages and I just never knew about it. But now that I do know, I want answers. I want to be prepared." I grabbed my iPad from the kitchen counter and settled down on the couch. "What did you say to Johnson when you saw him?"

Jake grinned. "I thought I did a pretty good acting job if I may say so myself. I walked by then did a double-take near the car. Knocked on his window, looked surprised to see him. Asked him what he was doing here. Johnson told me he was on his way home when he got a call from his boss, and he pulled over to take some notes. I told him it was nice to see him and continued on."

"He left a couple minutes after that."

"I guess I spooked him."

"Still, it wasn't super smart of him to go straight to Lily. Though maybe he organized to meet her in advance. Who knows? I don't think he realized I followed him. Okay, there were no profiles for him on Facebook, but I think I just found his Instagram account. Am I so old now that the kids aren't using the same social media sites as I am?"

Jake chuckled. "Maybe don't go booking yourself a room in that nursing home just yet."

I scrolled through the photos on his Instagram. He didn't post all that much, usually just a photo every few weeks. The most recent was a selfie taken at a club, so I confirmed that the account actually did belong to him.

"It looks like he boxes in his spare time," I said. "Oh, and here's a post where he's been promoted. Apparently, he's one of the youngest detectives in the Metropolitan Police. That doesn't surprise me. He's probably twenty-three, maybe twenty-four."

"Yeah, that sounds about right."

"He has a sister who's at university up in Scotland. There isn't much else on here."

"I mean, he's not going to be posting pictures with Lily and then captioning exactly what she plans on doing with him to mess with her sister," Jake pointed out.

"I know. But a girl can dream."

"And your big dreams are one of the things I love about you. But in this particular case, I don't think it's going to become reality."

"You're right. Still, it's good to know. It looks like he didn't go to college at all. Went right to the police after graduating from high school. Grew up in London, so this is his home turf. I wonder how he got in with Lily."

"Keep looking. You never know what you'll find."

"Okay, I'll keep going through all this. You're right. I can't expect the answers to just jump out at me. There has to be something here. And if not, well, I'm going to keep looking into Johnson. I want to know why he's spying on Violet for Lily. Ultimately, it's her I'm worried about."

"That family has the weirdest dynamics."

"Are you surprised though? I mean, knowing Violet and all?"

Jake shook his head. "Not in the least."

I went to bed that night with my thoughts racing. Now I had two cases to think about. There was Jeremy's murder, of course. But now a police detective was following Violet and reporting back to her sister. This was not good.

Chapter 11

I woke up early the next morning and walked Biscuit and Sequoia together before getting ready for another day of hunting down a killer. I was making coffee when I received a text from Violet.

We have been invited to join Sid and some other important people in his suite at the tennis today. We must leave here by ten. Dress nicely.

Experiencing Wimbledon in one of the fancy suites was certainly going to be an experience. I popped a bagel into the toaster as Jake wandered into the kitchen.

"Coffee?" I offered, grabbing the pot. He nodded as he came over to give me a quick peck on the cheek.

"Sounds great, thanks."

"Are you working today?"

"Sure am. I'm hoping to get the toxicology

report back on your body. I put a rush on it, and I'm hoping when the lab saw the name, they got the overnight shift to do it. Or however it works over there. I'm really not sure. How about you?"

"Well, not to make you jealous as you spend the entire day underground, but Violet texted that we've got a spot in one of the suites at Wimbledon today. So I guess I'm going to go watch some tennis and hopefully catch a murderer."

"Oh, that's great. That'll be a lot of fun. Well, not the murder part. But the tennis part."

"I hope so. I've never actually seen a tennis match live before."

"You're in for a treat, then. And I bet the seats they give you at the suite will be amazing. It's still first round, right?"

I nodded. "Yup, the last of the matches. Tomorrow's the start of the second. I guess that's why we got the invite. Sid won't want to have ponied up for us when the *real* games start."

"But he sure gets to look innocent by looking like he wants to help you find the killer, doesn't he?" Jake said wryly.

"Yup. I've certainly thought of that as well. If we were cops, it would be a total conflict of interest. But luckily, we can totally accept bribes of suite tickets at the tennis."

"Lucky you."

"That said, Sid is still one of our main suspects.

And you know Violet. It's not like she's going to let this affect her views of the case."

"No, for sure."

My bagel popped out of the toaster, and I began spreading jam on it while Jake poured himself a bowl of cereal. I sat down at the kitchen table and unlocked my phone. When I opened the news app and saw the biggest headline of the day, however, I dropped the bagel onto the plate in shock.

"What is it?" Jake asked.

I read from the phone. "Tennis Superstar Kristof Mayer Arrested for Murder."

"You're joking."

I continued to read the article below. "In the early morning hours, two detectives from London's Metropolitan Police arrived at the hotel where the Austrian tennis star is currently staying for the Wimbledon tournament. The superstar was heard shouting as detectives escorted him off the property, and reports have come out this morning that the star player has been arrested for the murder of business magnate Jeremy Flagstaff, who was killed two nights ago at a private party."

"I thought you said it wasn't Kristof."

"I don't think it is, not really," I said slowly. "He's… awful. There's no doubt about it. He deserves to rot in jail, but I don't think it should be for this."

"That should make your time at the tennis more interesting, at any rate."

"Yes," I said slowly. "In fact, I wonder if there hasn't been some behind-the-scenes meddling."

Jake raised an eyebrow. "You think Violet might be involved?"

"I might be wrong. I don't know. It could just be that the police have come to the wrong conclusion on their own. Or perhaps it's the right one. It could be me who's wrong. I'm not so up myself to think that I never make mistakes. I don't actually really know who killed Flagstaff. Either way, you're right about one thing. It will make today much more interesting."

AFTER EATING BREAKFAST, JAKE GOT READY TO GO to work, and I hopped onto Twitter to see if I could glean any more interesting tidbits about Kristof's arrest. Unfortunately, it was mostly filled with hot takes from people who thought he was too good a tennis player to throw in jail or conspiracy theories from people who thought the English wanted El to win so badly that they'd thrown one of his biggest opponents in jail to keep him from the tournament.

I did find grainy phone camera footage of Kristof's arrest. And I will admit, I felt a bit of petty satisfaction when I pressed play and watched the guy who had threatened us and attacked Violet yesterday being led off in cuffs.

The camera operator had been standing outside the Plaza hotel, where the tennis players were staying during the tournament. It was dark, the only illumination coming from the hotel windows and a few nearby streetlights. Initially, the only people visible in the frame were silhouettes, but it was easy to tell who was who. The two men flanking Kristof walked briskly, with the energy of police officers doing their job, as they dragged the taller man between them. Kristof kept trying to stop, shouting something incoherent. As he got closer to the camera, though, his words became more pronounced.

"You can't do this! I am innocent! Don't you know who I am? I'm Kristof Mayer. I'm the best tennis player in the world. You're going to pay for this. You'll be kicking homeless people out of parks until the day you retire, mark my words."

I bit back a smile as Kristof was dragged closer and closer to the unmarked police car. It was as if he realized what was really happening, and he fought more and more the closer he got. The person with the camera became bolder and walked toward the group.

"Holy crap, that's Kristof Mayer," the person recording said when they got close. "The tennis player! Hey, Rob, this video's going to go viral. Just you wait."

Well, they weren't wrong.

"This is bull! I'm going to sue! I have rights

under the Geneva Convention!" Mayer was still shouting as the detectives closed the door on him.

When the door finally closed, DCI Fletcher shot DCI Johnson a look that said, "I'm not looking forward to getting in that car and driving back to the station listening to him."

Then the two officers turned, got into the car, and sped off. A moment later, the video ended.

I had no idea how Kristof getting arrested was going to affect this case. Was he actually the guilty party? The police had to believe they had some evidence against him, and solid evidence too. They were going to get raked over the coals if they had to release him after the tournament.

Next thing I knew, it was coming up on ten o'clock, and I got myself ready to go. After giving the animals a quick pat and making sure they were all stocked up on water, I headed off to Violet's place. She met me at the front door, and the two of us began walking to Gloucester Road station, where the District Line trains offered a direct route to the stadium.

I still wasn't entirely used to trains being just as efficient as cars, but on a busy morning like this, it was actually faster to take the train than to try and grab a taxi or drive Jake's car. Plus it was far less stressful. There was something to be said for efficient public transport.

"I take it you've seen the news?" I said to Violet as we walked to the train station.

She gave me an enigmatic smile. "Indeed I have. He is not the killer, but it would do him good to have to spend some time in prison. He will miss the tournament and lose out on the prize money, but he only has himself to blame."

"Why do I have a feeling you've got a hand in this?"

"It is because I do. Kristof Mayer is an arrogant man who believes that none of his actions will ever have any consequences. Well, I have now shown him the consequence that comes along with making an enemy of Violet Despuis."

"What did you do?" I asked with a laugh.

"I planted evidence that he purchased cyanide on the dark web and then submitted an anonymous tip to the police," Violet replied with a shrug. "And believe me, Kristof Mayer's day is going to get much, much worse before it gets better."

I raised my eyebrows. "Oh?"

"You will see," she replied with a smile. "Although I admit, it was not entirely offense at Mayer's behavior yesterday that caused me to take this action. I wanted to have something big happen, something that would cause the players in this game to do react. I want to see all of their reactions now that a big play has been made. Normally, I would not have an innocent person arrested. But I do believe Mayer should spend some time in prison, so I have no problem with it in this particular instance."

"Remind me to never get on your bad side," I said as we reached the station entrance.

Ten minutes later, we were on a train, speeding toward Wimbledon. "So, how long are you planning on keeping Kristof in jail for a crime he didn't commit?"

Violet smiled. "We will see. Likely not long. I want to see the reactions of a few people to this news. Namely, Sid."

"Right. Well, seeing as he's the host of this whole shebang, we should find out. What's the other bad thing that's going to happen to Kristof? Don't tell me you've organized to have him shanked by somebody on day one."

"Oh, I would never be so crude as to do something like that. No. Kristof is going to discover that money can cover up many problems, but that only works until you have offended someone with more money than you. But it will be a few hours before you see what else I have planned. I want that news to land while we are watching the match."

"Everyone will be watching the tennis while you're at your own table at the back, playing chess."

"Yes, that is an excellent way of putting it. The pieces are in play, and I have made my move, and now I simply need to see how my opponent reacts before I take another step."

"Speaking of people being weird and mysterious, DCI Johnson is working for your sister. I followed him last night, and he met with her."

Violet raised her eyebrows. "Now that is interesting."

"Is that it? It's interesting?"

"Yes. What else do you want me to say? I know nothing about it. And it does not matter. Lily can live her own life. I am certain it is not the first time she has had me followed, and it will likely not be the last."

I couldn't say I was surprised by the answer. Violet wasn't the kind to let people in on this sort of thing. She could play it off as being nothing, but I knew she would be pulling strings behind the scenes.

I wasn't going to let it go, either. I'd seen DCI Johnson staking out our street. I saw him meet with Lily. There was something there. I was going to find out what.

But first, we had a murder to solve.

Chapter 12

We arrived at the All England Lawn Club once more, passed through security, and were directed up to the Skyview Suites. There, a woman dressed in a pretty foliage-print dress led Violet and me to the suite.

The Skyview Suites were gorgeous. Two long tables, each with plush chairs for ten, were set up with name tags so that each guest knew where to sit. At the far end of the tables, French doors opened wide to allow access to a balcony draped with greenery over which to look at the crowd below. The wall to the left was painted a beautiful pale green, with tennis legend Martina Navratilova's name printed in silver lettering. The suite was named for her, I supposed.

Around us milled about fifteen people. Sid was on the balcony, deep in conversation with a woman. Simon was here as well, munching on some canapés while chatting with another man dressed in a full suit, even in this early-summer heat.

A server dressed in the same foliage sundress as the one who had brought us here immediately approached Violet and me and offered us glasses of champagne.

Violet shook her head no, but I took one, and Violet cocked an eyebrow.

"What, you think two people in a week are going to have their champagne glasses tampered with?" I said with a wink, taking a sip.

"All right, perhaps I do not," Violet admitted. "Still, I avoid the champagne. Today, I want my mind to be sharp. I have made my play, and it is time to see how Sid reacts."

I followed her to the balcony, where the two of us looked out over the crowd.

After about five minutes, Sid addressed us. "Ah, Violet and Cassie. My two favorite detectives. I'm so glad you're here. You must have heard by now that Kristof was arrested for my poor friend's murder. Kristof. You know, I always knew something about that man was bad news. And of course, it's going to cause even more issues for us. Not that I mean to be callous about things, but I have a company to run. There are thousands of people whose jobs would be affected if I happened to lead the company astray over my grief. I have a responsibility to those people, as much as I did to Jeremy. Only I can't do anything for Jeremy now. But I can still do something for them."

"So, what is it that you will be doing?" Violet asked in a quiet voice. "I assume you will be going through with the termination of Kristof Mayer's contract?"

"Of course, yes. We were going to before. The wheels had already been set in motion, and especially in light of this new information, there's no way we can turn back on that plan. Just no way. Not that we would have, but now it's impossible."

"And will you be replacing him with El the way Jeremy wanted?"

"No. I don't think that would be prudent at all. He's just not the kind of person we want for the brand. Nothing against him, of course. He's just not right for Victory Shoes. However, don't tell anyone, but I'm speaking with Emily Connors's new agent next week. I'm sure we can come to a great deal, and Emily is young, which means she has a long career ahead of her. If she can stay healthy and continue to dominate, it could be huge for both of us."

"That is excellent. I am very happy for you. I do have one question: you were spotted arguing with Jeremy in the men's room the night that Jeremy was murdered. What was that about?"

Sid sighed. "It was about El. Jeremy wanted to tell him that night that we weren't going to sign him, as he'd just spoken to Emily Connors, and we had her lined up as soon as she found an agent. I disagreed. I thought it would be prudent to wait until the following day. After all, it was a party, not a business meeting. But Jeremy wanted to get it over and done with. He was always so impatient. That was one of his problems. Timing is everything in business."

"You threatened him," Violet said.

"Yes. Okay, I admit I did. But I didn't kill him. Kristof did. That was just how Jeremy and I spoke. We knew each other well. And I had to be tough with him. He had an ego. You don't get to be Jeremy Flagstaff without having an arrogant streak. So sometimes, I had to be tough to rein it in. But I had to do it for our business. Anyway, it's all moot. Kristof killed him. The police have arrested him."

"Yes, they have," Violet replied. "I just wanted to tie up all the loose ends for my own peace of mind."

"Right. Well, sometimes in business, you just don't get all of the answers." I resisted the urge to roll my eyes at the patronizing undertone in Sid's voice. "But in this case, that's what we were arguing about. It didn't matter, anyway. He told El that night despite my threats. That's what the two were arguing about."

"Now that is interesting," Violet said. "Thank you very much."

"Of course. Now, if you'll excuse me, I have other people to see."

"Just one more thing," Violet said quietly.

Sid paused. "Yes?"

"Is there anything you want to tell me about this case? Something that is not as it should be, perhaps? Something you want to get off your chest? Remember, I am one of the best detectives in the world. I am not the kind of person who will be fooled by tricks."

Sid's face went white. "What does it matter? Kristof has been arrested."

"It matters because he may not have done it. It matters because as far as I am concerned, the case is not over. Now, do you have something to tell me or no?"

Sid licked his lips and looked around as if trying to make a decision. He leaned toward us and lowered his voice. "I found a vial of cyanide in my office. The next day, okay? It was hidden in one of my plants. Not well, mind you. I have no idea where it came from. I promise you with every ounce of my being that I have never bought a vial of the stuff myself. But it was there. And I don't know how it got there."

"Your office, it is locked?"

"It was in the reception area. That part is open basically all day. There's usually my secretary around, but if she goes to get coffee or to the bathroom, then yes, it's open and empty. I don't have security cameras there, either. I want to maintain a certain level of class, you know? Why would I need them?"

"No, why indeed?" I asked dryly.

"Look, I couldn't have known that someone was going to plant poison in my office. And I'm telling you this because I'm innocent. I know how it looks. I know what it means. But I didn't do it."

"Where is the vial now?"

"Bottom of the Thames. I wasn't about to hang onto it."

Violet frowned. "Now, that is disappointing."

"Look, I'm sure whoever left it there didn't do it by accident. They were trying to frame me."

"What you see as nothing is often what I see as evidence," Violet replied. "Thank you for telling us about the vial."

"Someone is trying to ruin my life. And it's the same person who killed Jeremy. You have to stop them. I'm begging you."

"Go. Enjoy your day. Do not worry yourself too much. I am on the case."

Sid wandered off, and I leaned against the bar behind us, watching him go. "It's a good thing you waited until after you got the invitation to have Kristof arrested. I have a sneaking suspicion we're only here because Sid thought he was still a suspect, and he wanted to woo us."

Violet nodded. "Yes, indeed. It is interesting to see his reaction. And that he told us about the vial without me specifically mentioning it. He threw it out before the cops arrived, but I suspect the phone call the police received was real. Now, who left it?"

Sid walked over to someone else, but I spotted him glancing back at Violet a couple of times.

"He's not sure what to make of your questions. He's worried," I said. "He knows you aren't convinced Kristof is the killer. And that puts him right at the top of the suspect list. After all, he had a good reason to want Jeremy dead. He's telling you about the vial, but what if it's a lie? What if it existed, but he got rid of it because he's the killer? And now he's trying to make himself look set up."

"Indeed. And he should be worried. Because there is certainly a lot of evidence against him."

I shook my head. "Well, I'm hoping we're not having lunch with a killer, but who knows?"

The meal began shortly afterward. Four courses, all of them excellent, were served. Violet and I were seated as far from Sid as was possible, which I was sure wasn't an accident, but I had a nice chat with the woman sitting next to me, whose granddaughter wanted to go into medicine. However, we also spoke a little bit about Jeremy's murder.

"It's unconscionable, really. I feel so awful for that poor man. He has two daughters, did you know? Teenagers. One is seventeen and the other fifteen. Now they're going to have to bury their father right in the middle of the most tumultuous period of their lives. It's just sad."

"It really is. Those poor girls."

"And of course, Sid is putting on a brave face, but he's not handling it well, either. We've known each other since school, you know. Other than my husband, there isn't a man in the world I know better than Sid. He's out here doing what he has to do, but I know inside, he's in pain."

"It must be difficult for him."

"Yes. But he's always been the type to put his business ahead of his own personal needs. No matter what they are. It cost him his first marriage, about twenty years ago. His wife felt neglected— and this isn't me blaming her; she *was* neglected— and finally had enough. She told Sid it was either his business or her. And he chose the business. But I suppose ultimately, Sid needed someone who understood that he put money ahead of everything else, and Vanessa just wasn't that. She's happy now though. She's married to an accountant. Not nearly as rich as she would be if she'd stayed with Sid, but she's got someone who pays attention to her, and she values that so much more."

"That's nice for her."

"Indeed. And Sid is happy too. He never remarried, which I think is best for everyone. I don't think he ever wanted to. It was more that he felt obligated, that getting married was one of the boxes of life one was expected to tick off. And once he did it, that was enough. He's very much the definition of someone who's married to his work."

I didn't want to ask the woman directly if she

thought Sid could be the killer. After all, the case was supposed to be closed, and I figured that if she suspected me of thinking her friend a murderer, she'd probably stop talking to me. Not that I would blame her for that.

When our meal was finished, the afternoon games were just about to begin.

I checked my phone before heading out to the viewing area. "You said you had something else happening, right?" I asked Violet.

"Indeed," she replied. "It should not be long now. But come, enjoy the tennis while we wait."

The first match happening at Center Court that day was the first-round battle between El and a young athlete from France, who looked slightly nervous about facing the English star but was obviously trying to psych himself up for their upcoming battle.

The match was exciting, with El winning in five sets, keeping the crowd on the edges of their seats despite it being a first-round matchup. It was interesting that it was so close; perhaps the events of the last couple of days were weighing on El's mind.

After the match, Violet and I thanked Sid again and left, and as we were heading out, I checked my phone for news. When I saw the headlines, I let out an exclamation of surprise.

"Wow. You found footage of Kristof assaulting that woman?" I said. I clicked on a news story and pressed play on the camera footage that was listed after reading a warning about the violence in the video.

The footage was somewhat grainy, as the club's interior had been dark, but there was no doubt about it: that was Kristof on the footage. He was in what appeared to be some sort of closed-off VIP section of the club with a man I didn't recognize. Between them was a bottle of champagne, which Kristof took a swig from. A moment later, a woman arrived, obviously a waitress. Kristof tried to convince her to sit with him, but she smiled and motioned that she had to get back to the bar. He stood up and wrapped his arm around her waist, but the woman quickly stepped backward out of his reach.

Kristof frowned and began to yell. The woman said something to him, and Kristof leaned forward and punched her. She fell to the ground, and a moment later, a man leapt into the frame and dragged Kristof out of view of the camera.

"There's no doubt about it," I said, shaking my head. "What a complete tool. You're right, he deserves to spend some time in jail, even if it's technically for a crime he didn't commit."

"He did not, I am certain of that."

"Wait, you've solved it?"

"Oh, yes. Now, it is just about proving it."

"How did you get the camera footage?"

"Everybody has their price. I found the woman Kristof hurt. It was not difficult. I found out from her that she had gotten the footage from her place of employment. I offered her enough money that she could return the bribe to Kristof Mayer and have a couple million euros left over."

My eyes widened. "You paid her millions of euros for her story?"

"I am fortunate enough to be able to do so easily, yes. And while I know some may argue that it was a waste of money, that there are better things to spend it on, I disagree. As far as I am concerned, Kristof Mayer is a horrible human being who should be exposed for what he has done, not to ruin his reputation—although that will happen—but to protect others by giving them a warning when they encounter him. Besides, I told him not to push me, and he decided to push. Now, he discovers that there are consequences to one's actions in life."

I laughed. "Wow. You were not kidding. First, you get him thrown in jail for a crime he didn't commit just to see how the other suspects react, and then you pay millions of dollars to make sure the world knows he's an abuser and his reputation is ruined forever? Remind me to never get on your bad side," I said again.

Violet laughed. "Do not worry, there is no risk of that. You are not inherently a terrible human being."

"I do my best. Anyway, we haven't spoken enough about you knowing who the killer is. Who did it?"

"I cannot say yet. I am still puzzled. I need to find out how to prove it."

"You're not going to give me a little hint?" I asked with a smile.

"I am sorry, but no. You will have to wait if you have not analyzed the same clues I saw for yourself."

Some things never changed.

Chapter 13

On the way home from the tennis, I got a phone call from a number I didn't recognize.

"Hello?" I answered.

"Hi, is this Doctor Coburn?"

"Yes, speaking."

"This is Margaret Anderson calling from Chelsea and Westminster Hospital. Fatima gave me your name. I'm afraid I've got a shortage of doctors working tonight, and I'm wondering if you'd like to take a shift. If you can't, it's no worries. I'll manage. But I'd really appreciate it if you're available. My apologies for the short notice."

I was hit with a sudden wave of tiredness, which I shook off. "When would you like me to start?"

"Would ten o'clock tonight work?"

"That should be fine," I said, mentally chiding

my brain that we were at least going to get a few hours' rest in before having to work.

"I'm very glad to hear it. Thank you, Doctor. I'll see you soon."

I said goodbye to Margaret and ended the call.

"Taking on another shift?" Violet asked.

I nodded. "Might as well. You know who the killer is and have to come up with a plan, so why not get some work in while I wait for that to happen? It's not like there's going to be much else exciting happening with this case anytime soon."

"That is true."

"The more I work in the hospital, the more I enjoy it. It's not surgery, that is true. I've had to come to terms with the fact that that's never going to be my life. But emergency is nice. It's detective work in a way. You can talk to the patients more; they're not under anesthetic. So you have to figure out what they're telling you, what's going on between the lines."

"I am glad. It is good for you to have something like that in your life. It is one thing to help me with investigations, but I know it is not what you truly want to do for yourself."

"No," I admitted. "I'm not as good at it as you are anyway."

"Nobody is."

I smiled at the simple way Violet said those words then stifled a yawn. "If I was, then I'd know who you have in mind."

"You will know soon enough. I will find my proof."

"I don't doubt it."

As soon as I got home, I took the two animals for a quick walk around the block, left a note for Jake letting him know I was working that night at Chelsea and Westminster, and crawled into bed to get a few hours of sleep before my shift. I set my alarm for nine o'clock, and when I woke up and made my way into the living room, Jake was watching TV with the cat on his lap and Sequoia leaning against him, snoring away.

"You look comfortable," I said with a smile as I headed to the kitchen to get a bit of food before I was on my way.

"The animals have chosen me as a great place to cuddle," Jake said with a shrug. "I'm stuck here until they move, which I'm pretty sure isn't going to be until the morning. But that's all right. I've accepted my fate."

I laughed. "Great. I'm going to find something to eat."

"There's leftover spaghetti if you want it."

"That sounds great."

"Have you worked at that hospital before?"

I shook my head. "Nope. It'll be new. But I mean, it's accident and emergency. It's always new.

The only thing that's different is the layout of the place. I never know what to expect."

"That's true. Well, I hope tonight is a good one for you."

"I hope so too. I could use an exciting night. I want something to get my thoughts away from this case. And from the whole situation with DCI Johnson. I have to think about what I'm going to do about that. You were right. Violet isn't worried at all. But I don't like it."

"You should follow your instincts, I think. I know Violet knows a lot, and this is her life and her sister, but your instincts are good too. If something is telling you to look into this, then you should do that."

I nodded. "I will. I think Lily is up to something, and whatever it is, I don't like it. But there's nothing I can do about it right now. Although I will be checking on my way out if DCI Johnson is parked on our street again. And if he is…" I shook my fist threateningly.

Jake laughed. "You tell him."

"We can carpool to the emergency room."

At nine-thirty, Jake drove me down to the hospital. We didn't spot DCI Johnson at the end of our street. It was late enough at night that there wasn't much traffic at all, and Jake was able to park right in front of the accident and emergency doors.

I gave him a kiss and went in for my shift. Margaret, who ran the floor, turned out to be a plump woman in her fifties with an efficient manner and an easy smile. She had worked as a doctor for more than twenty years and was happy to give me a quick tour and introduce me to the other doctors I'd be working with that evening.

"Thank you for coming in on such short notice. I'm running a skeleton staff to begin with, and when we had three people call in sick—they all went to the same sketchy restaurant for lunch yesterday and ended up with food poisoning—I didn't know what I was going to do. Then Fatima told me about you and gave me your number."

"Of course. I'm happy to help. I generally just do shifts here and there in between my other work."

Margaret nodded. "I've seen you in the papers. You work with Violet Despuis. She's fantastic. A wonderful detective. I love reading all about the cases she solves."

"Life is never boring when she's around."

"I bet. Now, let's get you sorted for the night."

Before I knew it, I'd been given a tour of the ward and a pager and was ready to go.

My first patient of the night was a man in his late sixties, maybe early seventies, who had had an accident while trying to do some home renovations on his own. He'd stepped on a large nail, which went straight through his foot, boot and all, and was sticking out the top of it.

The craziest part was that he walked himself right into A&E and politely informed the triage nurse of his injury as if he'd simply gotten a slight graze on his knee.

When he told her he'd stepped on a nail, she stood up to have a look and immediately called for more nurses.

The man was loaded into a wheelchair and then into a bed, where I was called in to have a look.

"This is Doctor Coburn," the nurse informed him, shooting me a smile. "Doctor, this is Alan. He's presented with a large nail protruding through his foot and through his shoe."

I looked down at Alan's foot. Sure enough, he had been wearing a pair of black boots that now had a six-inch nail poking straight up through the top, around three-quarters of the way to his toes. The top fabric of his shoe was lightly stained a deep rust color, but on the bright side, the nail appeared to be keeping most of his blood inside his body.

"Well, Alan, on a scale of one to ten, how much does it hurt?" I asked.

"It's probably a six. It's not too bad, really. Back in seventy-two, I fell off a ladder at me mum's house, trying to fix up her gutters. Landed on me back, fractured two vertebrae. Now *that* one hurt. Not the broken bones but the scolding I got from Mum when she heard I climbed up the ladder by myself without anyone to hold it. To be fair, I was twenty-two, and all my brain cells hadn't quite grown in. I'd like to think I'm a bit smarter these days, but then again, if I were, I wouldn't be sitting here now, would I?"

I immediately liked Alan. He had a thin frame and big blue eyes that glimmered with amusement, surrounded by wrinkles that betrayed a lot of smiling in life. His nose and lips were thin, and he wore a simple brown sweater, which looked as if it had probably been knitted in the seventies, over a plain gray T-shirt. His head was bald save for a few scraggles of white hair desperately hanging on.

"We all make mistakes," I said with a smile. "All right. I'd like to start off by going in for X-rays if you can handle the pain of the nail still being in there. I'd like to see what we're working with in terms of the bone situation before we take it out."

"You're the doctor, so whatever you think sounds good to me," he said with a wink.

"All right, let me just put the order in, and someone from radiology will be here shortly to take care of you. And if you change your mind about those drugs, you let one of the nurses know, okay?"

"I will."

The fact that he wasn't in so much pain that he needed drugs told me there was a good chance he'd missed the bones. Odds were the nail had gone between two of his metatarsals, but I was going to have to get that boot off to know for sure. And while I wasn't one hundred percent sure what Alan's mobility levels were, I wanted him to have the best chance at continuing to use that foot normally for as long as possible.

While I waited for Alan's X-rays to come back, I took care of another patient. This one was a pretty easily diagnosable case of appendicitis; between the fever, the pain at McBurney's point, and the nausea, I felt pretty confident sending the patient off to the OR, where a surgeon would be ready and waiting to remove the appendix before it burst.

When I checked back at the main station, the X-rays were ready. I had a quick look. Sure enough, the nail was right between the second and third metatarsals on Alan's left foot. This shouldn't be too difficult.

Chapter 14

I headed back to Alan's room. "I've got your X-rays back, Alan, and it looks like we're ready to remove the nail, if that's all right with you. Is there a medical reason you'd rather avoid the pain medication?"

"No," Alan replied, shaking his head. "I'm not allergic or a junkie or anything like that. It's just I've never liked putting stuff in my body that I didn't understand. I've always avoided drugs when I can."

"Okay. If it's all right with you, I'd like to apply a local anesthetic to your foot. It will hurt, but not nearly as much as removing the nail without anything for the pain would."

"If you think it's best. I will admit, sitting here, it is beginning to hurt."

"I'm not surprised. When was the last time you received a tetanus shot?"

"I live in London, not Lincolnshire. It's been at least twenty years."

"As you've just found out, London has rusty nails as well. I'll give you a booster, then, as it's been more than ten years. Now, here's how we're going to do this. I'm going to take the laces out of your boot and cut your sock so I can access your skin and give you the anesthetic. Then I'm going to take the nail out and immediately remove your boot and sock so that I can stem the bleeding."

"Wait, hold on," Alan interrupted, suddenly looking worried. "You can't take off my boot."

I paused, frowning slightly. "Why not?"

"You just… you can't. You just can't. I need it to stay on."

"Can you tell me why? Because I promise you, whatever it is, I've seen worse. I'm an ER doctor. Believe me." I didn't add that they don't tell you in medical school that a large part of this job involves pulling items from people's rectums that absolutely do not belong there.

Still, Alan shook his head. "No. No, I'm afraid that's not possible. Can't you just remove the nail and then give me some bandages, and I'll be on my way? I'll be fine, I promise. This isn't the worst thing that's ever happened to me."

"I'm afraid I can't," I said as gently as I could. "I need to make sure your foot is fine. You might never be able to walk properly again if it doesn't heal correctly."

"That's fine. I'll take that risk."

There was something weird going on. Why didn't Alan want me to see his foot? I mean, sure, I could understand people being self-conscious about their feet. It happened all the time. And while I didn't care what they looked like, that didn't stop people from wanting to avoid showing me the body parts they were sensitive about. But to continue to refuse after I told him the potential consequences involved never walking again? No, something weird was going on here.

"Can we compromise?" I offered. "What if I take off your boot, but I only cut your sock off enough to keep your toes covered? Would that be acceptable?"

Allen breathed a visible sigh of relief. "I can live with that. But you have to promise you're not going to try and have a look at my toes."

"I promise." And I meant it. Just because I was a doctor didn't mean that I should have unfettered access to somebody's body, and even though I was curious as anything, I wasn't about to do something that Alan wasn't comfortable with. Especially something he specifically asked me not to do.

"Okay," he said. "Do what you have to do."

I set about getting my equipment ready, and Alan turned back into the talkative old man he had been before we started the conversation about his toes.

"So you're what we call a Yank if my ears don't

deceive me. Of course, at my age, my entire body feels like it's playing one big practical joke on me. But I'm pretty sure I've got this one right."

"You certainly do. I grew up in San Francisco," I replied as I prepared the anesthetic.

"What brought you to London then?" Alan asked.

"You could call it a quarter-life crisis. Probably the best crisis of my life."

"I've lived in a lot of places over the years. And you know, there's something that always brings me back to London. As far as decisions made in crisis go, this was not a bad place to end up."

"I agree with you, Alan. London is one of the greatest cities in the world. Although I haven't lived in nearly as many places as you by the sound of it."

"If you get the opportunity when you're young, I highly recommend it. Even if you just travel as a tourist. You're in England. The entire world is at your fingertips. Flights are so cheap now, you can go explore so many places that were difficult to access when I was a lad. Why would you not travel to the Mediterranean for a long weekend one day, just because you can? Oh, there is such a huge world out there for you to see."

"My boyfriend took me to Rome for a weekend once," I said with a nostalgic smile. "That was a year or so ago."

"He sounds like a very sensible young man."

"That he is. Now, let me cut the laces on your

boot here, Alan." I took the scissors and began my careful movements.

"Just be careful with the sock, please," Alan said, his voice tinged with nervousness.

"Don't worry, I've got it," I said with a wink to help him relax. "Now, most doctors will tell you this needle won't hurt a bit," I said once I'd cut the sock down to the wound and pried it all apart so that I could see his skin.

"Oh, I've had this done before. I'm well aware that's a lie."

"Good. You're right, it is a lie. It will hurt. But pulling out that nail without any anesthetic would hurt a lot more. On the bright side, it should only be painful for a few seconds before the anesthetic starts to kick in. Are you ready?"

"Yes, ma'am."

I poked the needle through his skin and pressed on the plunger to send the anesthetic into his body. Alan inhaled sharply, but after a moment or two, he began to relax. When I was finished, I crouched in front of his foot to get a good look at the nail I was about to remove. It was really lodged in the bottom of his boot.

"How did you say this happened again?"

"I was doing some renovations at my place. I must have left a nail lying around that I didn't notice, because I was just getting ready to go to bed when I felt pain shoot through my foot. I looked down, and what do you know, I'm staring at the business end of a six-inch nail."

"Okay. I'm going to pull this out now. I'm not going to yank, but you're going to feel consistent pressure."

"You do what you have to."

I nodded and began to pry the nail out with my fingertip. When it had been moved out about half an inch, I grabbed the end and pulled gently but firmly, making sure I had the angle right so that the nail would come straight out while doing minimal damage.

Sure enough, the nail slid back out the way it had gone, and I immediately jumped into action. After all, now that the nail was out, the wound was going to start bleeding, and fast.

I removed the rest of Alan's boot, and I pulled back the rest of the sock, leaving his toes covered. He watched me carefully as I grabbed a number of gauze pads and cleaned the wound thoroughly before inspecting the hole in his foot. It was clean, and it didn't look like an infection had set in yet, which was a promising sign. Of course, Alan wasn't totally out of the woods yet. An open wound, especially one of that size, could easily get infected as it healed, especially when it was located on the bottom of the foot, a part of the body that very easily came into contact with dirt and other particles that could enter the body.

"So, what's the prognosis, doctor?" he asked.

"Am I going to walk out of here on my own two feet?"

"You sure are," I said with a smile. I avoided looking at the toes he was so sensitive about. "I'm going to wrap this up for you, and I'm going to give you a course of oral antibiotics to take just in case. I want you to replace the bandages every three days, and wash the wound clean when you do so. Please wear clean socks and shoes everywhere, including in the house. I know that goes against every instinct you have as a British person, but trust me, it's important in this case."

"I think I can manage that. I'll have to go buy a new pair of shoes in the morning though. This one seems to have been ruined," he said, ruefully shooting a glance at the boot that now lay abandoned on the floor, a hole passing through the sole and through the tongue, stained with blood. "Any chance you can find me something to wear as I leave here? Maybe even just one of those puffy things you doctors wear over your real shoes?"

"I'll see what I can find. Now, let me just stitch you up then bandage up this wound, and I'll get you out of here."

"Great. Oh, you know, I am feeling a little bit of pain. Are there some drugs out there you can give me after all?"

"I'll have a nurse do it," I said with a smile.

Alan let out a small grunt and shifted on the bed. "Thank you very much. I appreciate the good work you've done here. You know, you should have been a surgeon. You seem to have a knack for stitching people up."

I smiled. "Maybe in another life." At the same time, when Alan shifted, something moved at the end of the bed and caught my eye. I glanced over as subtly as I could, not wanting Alan to notice me looking at the feet he was so sensitive about, and I had to hide my amazement.

It was a diamond. An honest-to-goodness diamond, sitting on the sheet of the hospital bed. How had that gotten there? It had obviously fallen out of the toe of Alan's sock. But why was he keeping precious gems in his footwear?

No one did that. Not a chance. Not unless they'd stolen them. I turned back to him, plastering a smile on my face and trying to pretend I hadn't seen anything. "I'm going to give you some silver mesh that I want you to place over the wound as well. Silver is a natural antibiotic. The mesh will add an extra layer of protection."

"That sounds like a plan."

"Now, while I finish up these stitches, why don't you tell me about your favorite place in the world to travel?" I suggested. I was hoping that if I got Alan lost in his memories, he might look away from his foot for a moment, and I could grab the diamond that was just sitting on the bed without his noticing it. I had so many questions, and I couldn't ask any of them.

"Have you ever been to Cairo? Best city on the planet, and it's not even close. I love it there. Everything is steeped in history. The pyramids are a short drive away. They're five thousand years old. It's incredible. You stand there in the middle of the Sahara, and you stare at them, knowing that you're looking on exactly the same thing as Napoleon did, as Julius Caesar did, as Cleopatra did. The exact same thing. It's astounding. And the city itself is chaotic. Very easy to lose yourself in, but I like that about a place. London is much more organized. For living long term, yes, give me London any day. But there's something about Cairo that just works. Go there if you can."

"I've been to Egypt. I agree with you. Have you seen Abu Simbel?"

"Oh, yes. Lovely place."

"It is. That was one of my favorite places in Egypt." I left out the part about being shot at by a thief. "It's very hot though. Oppressively so."

"Yes. It's certainly easy to understand where the myth of Helios's chariot falling too close to the earth and scorching the land came from."

Since Alan wasn't going to look away, I decided I was going to have to swipe the diamond while he was watching. I was going to have to be subtle about it. When I had him all patched up, I stood up, placing my hand over the diamond as I pretended to heave myself to my feet.

"All right, I think we're all set here," I said,

glancing at his socks. If I looked closely, I was fairly certain there were other protruding bits that shouldn't have been there. More diamonds?

"Great," Alan said quickly. "Thank you very much, Doctor Coburn."

"Please, call me Cassie."

I couldn't be sure, but I thought a flash of worry passed over his eyes then.

"Cassie it is."

I slipped the diamond into my pocket and turned away from Alan but eyed his reflection in the glass pane of the storage supply closet to see what he was doing. Sure enough, Alan was pulling something from the tip of his sock. It had to be more diamonds.

"So, am I putting this boot back on?" he asked me.

"I'd rather you didn't," I said. At the last second, I noticed Alan had stood up. He moved toward me, and I ducked out of the way just in time to avoid being hit over the head with an emesis basin—they called it a kidney dish over here in England. The stainless steel dish clanged against the wall, and he swore upon realizing he'd missed his target.

Great. I was being attacked by a seventy-something-year-old jewel thief. Never a boring night in A&E.

Chapter 15

Alan hurled the kidney dish at me and ran out of the room. I held my arms up to block it and swore as I followed him. He was quick and nimble, more so than I had expected, especially for a man with a hole in the bottom of his foot. As soon as I entered the hallway, I looked around, but I'd completely lost sight of him.

Swearing, I went back into the trauma room and called for security. I wanted Alan caught before he left the premises, although the most important thing was that he didn't hurt anybody else in this hospital. When security was called, I texted Violet.

Do you know of any older diamond thieves? In their seventies, maybe? Because I think one just ran away from me at the hospital.

As soon as I sent the text, I went back into the hall. I had to find Alan. Where could he have gone? I forced myself to pause and think about this instead

143

of panicking. I was an emergency room doctor. Keeping my head level when everything around me was going nuts was an essential part of my job.

I paused, took a deep breath, and looked around. To the immediate left was a stairwell. I entered it, my eyes scanning for a clue. I found it on the handrail leading downstairs: a tiny smidge of blood, which probably got on Alan's hand when he grabbed the kidney dish full of bloody gauze and dumped it on the floor before trying to hit me with it.

I rushed down the stairs, my every sense on high alert. My skin tingled, and my throat felt like a boa constrictor had wrapped itself around it as I headed down to the basement level. There didn't appear to be too much down here; it seemed to mainly serve as a supply area for the rest of the hospital.

Still, Alan was down here somewhere, and I wasn't about to let him get away.

I crept through the dim hallway, my eyes adjusting to the light, on high alert. Behind me, I heard a sound. I turned to see someone wearing personal protective equipment and heading to the elevators, pushing a trolley full of medical instruments. Normally, I wouldn't have thought much of it, but I knew what a slight limp looked like. I knew it all too well, because I had one myself.

I turned and followed the person, who looked back. Sure enough, I recognized those blue eyes. It was Alan. I ran after him as soon as he recognized me. He grabbed a scalpel from the tray and pushed the rest of it toward me. I was really getting sick and tired of having medical equipment launched in my direction.

Flinging the cart aside with a crash, I swore and rushed after Alan. He had gone back for the stairs, and I followed him.

"Stop right there," I shouted at him.

"Not a chance, little lady. I don't care who your friends are. You're not getting your hands on me."

He must have recognized my name. Of course, a criminal would be well aware of Violet Despuis. He would have had to be. And if he'd looked into her a little bit, he would have come across my name as well, as I occasionally made it into the news articles about cases we'd worked together.

I caught up to Alan at the top of the stairs, and he lunged at me with the scalpel, but I grabbed his wrist. I mimicked the same move Violet had used against Kristof and twisted Alan's arm behind him. He let out a yelp of pain and dropped the scalpel, which I kicked out of the way.

"Now, you're going to explain to me where those diamonds came from," I said with a grunt, right as one of the security guards entered the stairwell.

As it turned out, Alan wasn't the man's real name. I could have figured that one out for myself though. Alan was his neighbor who had died a year earlier. Mortimer Gladwell, as it turned out the thief's real name was, had taken over the man's identity and used it when he needed to get services he didn't want connected to himself.

Mortimer Gladwell was a diamond thief and, by all accounts, a very good one. The fact that he didn't have a criminal record at all confirmed that. But Violet, who arrived on the scene within minutes, was able to link him to a half dozen unsolved diamond thefts. The police were called, and the DCI who responded told us that earlier that night, a diamond theft had been reported at a private residence on the other side of London, all the way in Greenwich. The thief had gotten away but stumbled over some construction equipment left by the tradies putting in a new kitchen for the owner.

"That must have been when he stepped on the nail," I said when this was explained.

"Right," DCI Evers agreed. She was in her thirties, with a friendly face and frizzy black hair tied back in a ponytail. "We believe he stepped on the nail, kept going, and made his escape. However, he must have realized he was going to need medical attention and figured that no one saw him step on the nail, so he wouldn't have had to worry too much. Still, he went to the other side of London to find a hospital nowhere near where the injury took place, and he used the identity of his old neighbor to be seen."

"He must have noticed that the diamond dropped out of his sock and that I took it. Then, when I told him my name, he put everything together," I said. "He knew I was going to report him or try and stop him, and he tried making another run for it."

"Luckily, this time, he was stopped," DCI Evers said. "Good work."

"I'm just glad no one else in the hospital was hurt."

"He is not a thief who takes to violence," Violet explained. "In all of the cases I have him linked to, he committed his crimes at night, when the victims were known to be away from home. He is a runner, not a fighter. But of course, one can never be certain what someone will do when they are cornered. I am glad that everyone is safe."

"Me too," I agreed. "That's ultimately the most important thing. The fact that Alan is sitting in a cop car and headed to jail is just a bonus."

"Your landlady will be pleased," Violet said with a smile.

"Oh? I should have known Mrs. Michaels would have known him."

"She did. In fact, if you bribe her with cookies, she might even tell you how she and Mortimer Gladwell were once engaged."

I raised my eyebrows. "Wow."

"He has been active for a very long time. I have been aware of him for years, but he is careful. He does not follow a pattern, and he often waits months, even years, between his different strikes. I was never able to find the evidence to put him away, but you have done that tonight."

"What I don't get is why hide the diamonds in his socks?" DCI Evers said. "Wouldn't it be easier to just shove them into his pockets or something?"

"It was an extra layer of security," Violet explained. "If he was caught outside a home that had been burgled, he would invite the police to search him quickly. They would find nothing, because who would look in a man's socks? They would then move on to try and find the real thief. It was simply insurance. However, he did not expect that this time around, his foot would plunge onto a nail that would pierce it entirely."

"And he couldn't get at the diamonds to remove them until I'd taken out the nail," I said, nodding. "That was also why he kept trying to get me to leave the room, I bet. He wanted to be able to get at the diamonds and put them in his pocket so that I wouldn't see them. But of course, I didn't. Not because I realized what he was doing but because as a doctor, I wasn't about to leave the room when he had an open wound."

"It is a good thing, that," Violet said. "Well, it has been a more exciting night than I anticipated."

The DCI nodded. "I'm going to head to the

station and do the paperwork. Would you mind joining me, Violet? I could use your expertise to nail down the other cases he's a suspect in. With your help, I think Mortimer is going to be spending the rest of his life in prison."

"I am happy to help."

Violet and DCI Evers took their leave, and I headed back to the main station, where Margaret was waiting for me. "I have a broken leg that just came in if you're finished with them."

"You got it," I replied. That was the thing about the emergency room. It didn't care what you had going on; there was always another patient ready and waiting.

By the time my shift ended, at six the next morning, I was completely exhausted. It had been an interesting night to say the least, and I was eternally grateful for Jake getting up early to come and pick me up.

I collapsed into the passenger seat of the car, where he handed me a hot cup of coffee.

"Have I ever told you how amazing you are?" I said gratefully. I wrapped my hands around the cup and took a sip, letting the hot liquid running down my throat soothe my body.

"Sure, but I always love to hear it. How did the night go?"

"Well, I managed to catch a jewel thief who hid diamonds in his sock before he stepped on a nail."

Jake raised his eyebrows. "Sometimes, I think you just make things up. That's the sort of thing that just doesn't happen to ordinary people. Only you."

"He tried to run away, but I caught him in the basement, and now the police have him. Violet is with the DCI, working out the charges. I'm sure she has enough proof of crimes he's committed to put him away for a long time."

"Your entire life is nuts."

"That's the ER life. When the bodies are still alive, they tend to do a bit more than just lie on the slab for you. Although generally, the saying is that the truly insane stuff happens during a full moon."

"You've got a couple weeks to go, then."

"Indeed."

Jake pulled the car away from the curb and began the drive back home. He glanced in the rearview mirror a couple times.

"What is it?"

"I think someone is following us."

I glanced in the side mirror and saw a pair of headlights belonging to the car behind us. "Oh yeah?"

"I just made two turns that weren't necessary, and they've followed us. Let me just pull over here and see if he goes past. Pull out your phone. I'm going to pretend to be looking at something on it, and you have a look at who it is."

Jake put his blinker on and pulled into a parking spot then leaned over and looked at my phone. I had my head down but glanced up to recognize the Peugeot that drove past.

"It's DCI Johnson," I said breathlessly.

Jake scowled. "I thought it might be. Well, let's see how he likes it."

He pulled out of the parking spot, but the car in front of us had disappeared. "I bet he turned off his lights," I said, glowering.

Jake sped up a bit and drove a few blocks, but DCI Johnson's car had disappeared.

"What do you want to do about him? He was obviously following you, and I don't like it."

"I'm going to talk to Superintendent Williams," I said. "After all, he's his boss. I want him to know what's going on. He would want to know. And then, I'm going to go back to the bar where I saw Lily the other day and see if I can find out anything about her. There's something happening here, and I want to know what it is. But first, sleep."

"That sounds like a good idea."

Jake drove home, and I got ready for bed while he prepared to go to work. "Are you going to be okay here?" he asked. "I don't know what DCI Johnson wants, but I'm worried about you being here alone. After all, he's been watching you."

"I'll be fine," I said. "I'll put the extra lock on

the door. He hasn't tried anything yet, and I don't know if he will. He seems to just be watching. I'll send Mrs. Michaels a text as well, just in case. She won't let anything happen if he comes by."

"Good thinking. Okay. Let me know if you need anything."

"Got it. Don't worry about me. I'm just going to sleep."

Jake gave me a quick kiss and headed off to work. I bolted the door behind him and went to bed. Despite my exhaustion, I spent quite a while lying on my back, staring at the ceiling, thinking over the million different things that seemed to be going on with my life.

Who had actually killed Jeremy Flagstaff? Why were Lily and DCI Johnson watching me and Violet? Was Alan—sorry, Mortimer—going to admit to what he'd done now that he had been caught?

Eventually, however, exhaustion took over, and I drifted off to sleep.

Chapter 16

When I woke up, sunlight was streaming through the window, and I groaned, grabbing my pillow and throwing it over my face to try and get back to sleep. But I knew it was pointless. I was awake. I couldn't sleep through the whole day anyway; it would throw off my entire circadian rhythm.

Instead, I glanced over at my phone, whose screen was on. I'd just gotten a text a few seconds ago, which must have been what woke me up.

It was from Violet.

I have made a decision regarding the killer. We will not be able to prove what I would like to prove without a confession. I have made plans. Are you willing to join me?

Sure. Just let me know when, I replied, glancing at the time. It was just after one. I'd slept for almost five hours, maybe. That wasn't too shabby.

It will be tonight. I will get you the details, but be prepared to leave here after six.

Roger that.

I dragged myself into the kitchen and poured myself a cup of coffee then decided on an action plan for the day. I was going to see Superintendent Williams and let him know what was going on with DCI Johnson, but I couldn't have him meet me at the station. After all, if DCI Johnson was there, he might figure out what I was up to.

So instead, I picked a coffee shop a few blocks away and texted the superintendent, asking if he could meet me there in an hour.

I can. Is the reason for this meeting something you can tell me by text?

I'd rather not. But it's important.

All right. I'll be there.

I had a shower and got changed then took the tube to the coffee shop I'd picked out. I ordered a latte then sat at a table where I'd be visible from the entrance.

A few minutes later, Superintendent Williams came and sat across from me. The higher rank was doing him good. His red hair was cut close, and he wore a suit and tie, which gave him a more professional appearance. Plus he carried himself with the confidence of a man who was moving up the ranks of his chosen career.

"Cassie," he said, sitting across from me. "It's good to see you. It's been too long."

"You too. You look good."

"Thank you. So do you. I heard you're working at the hospital now, in emergency."

"Yeah, I am. From time to time, anyway."

"So, what did you need to talk to me about?"

"It's one of your detectives. DCI Emmett Johnson. Do you mind telling me what the deal is with him?"

"Sure. He transferred here from Birmingham a few months ago. He doesn't have a lot of experience as a detective yet, but we all have to start somewhere. I've got him with Fletcher, who's perhaps not the sharpest tool in the shed, but he means well. Johnson is eager and willing to learn, which is always an advantage. Why do you want to know about him? Has he done something wrong?"

"He's been following me and Violet," I explained.

Superintendent Williams's eyebrows flew skyward. "Following you?"

"This morning, when I left the hospital, he tailed Jake and me back to our apartment. And a couple nights before that, he was parked at the end of our street. I followed him. He went and met Lily, Violet's sister, at a bar on the other side of town. He's obviously working for her. To what end, I don't know."

Superintendent Williams pursed his lips. "This is very serious. What would you like me to do?"

"For now, nothing. I don't want him alerted to the fact that I know about him."

"Have you spoken to Violet?"

I nodded. "She doesn't seem concerned. But I don't know. Something about this feels off to me, and I want to figure out what's going on. I wanted you to know too, just in case. But that said, don't do anything. Don't treat him any differently. I'll keep you in the loop of what I find out though."

"Good. The detectives working under me should be working for the people of this city and not just one of them in particular. I don't like this at all."

"You can't let him know right now," I said hurriedly. "Please."

"I won't. But only because you're the one asking. I'll keep this under wraps, but keep me informed. I'm willing to give you some leeway on this, but long term, if he's working for Lily, and especially if he's stalking you and Violet, I don't want him on my police force."

"What else can you tell me about him?"

Superintendent Williams shrugged. "Honestly? Not much. He came from another department. I called his old boss, who said he was a good worker. Smart. And he is that. He likes to think about cases, and he likes to tie up loose ends. Those are some signs of someone who's going to be a good detective. He always shows up on time, keeps his head down, and does his work. I haven't had any complaints. But he doesn't talk much about himself. Not at all, actually, come to think of it. I don't know where he grew up, if he has a girlfriend, what his family is like. Some police are like that, though, so I didn't think much of it. But now…"

"I have a sneaking suspicion anything he would have said is a lie anyway," I replied with a slight shrug. "It's fine. I just wanted to let you know what was going on."

"I appreciate that. I'll keep my eyes and ears open for you in case I hear anything. And Cassie?"

"Yeah?"

"Be careful. I know you always are, but I mean it. If you're being followed, it could end badly. Do you want me to order a squad car to drive by your place on its nightly rounds?"

I shook my head. "Thanks, but no. I don't want him to realize anything is up. Not while I'm looking into this."

"All right. Let me know if that changes."

"I will."

Superintendent Williams said goodbye and left. I drummed my fingers lightly along the table as I considered what he said. I had a feeling it wasn't an accident that DCI Johnson had virtually no history and wasn't a talker. He was trying to hide who he really was.

I was going to discover his true identity.

I left the coffee shop and took a train to St Paul's station, walking from there to the pub where I'd

SAMANTHA SILVER

seen DCI Johnson the other night. Technically, Blackfriars was closer, but it would have required an extra connection. Besides, it was a beautiful day, and after a long, dreary winter and a spring season that often felt so oppressive I wondered if we'd ever see the sun again, it was nice to get out and be able to stretch my legs and feel the sun on my face.

I entered the pub and found a round and red-faced man behind the bar. Red hair poked wildly from under his flat cap.

"Aye, what can I get ye?" he asked in a thick Scottish brogue when I sat myself at the bar.

"Whatever your favorite beer on tap is, please." I pulled out my phone and did a quick Google search, finding a picture of Lily. I showed it to the bartender. "She was in here the other night, around eleven, with a man. Do you recognize her?"

The bartender leaned in close, squinting at the screen. "Ah, yes. She was here. Never seen her before that night. Haven't seen her since."

"You wouldn't happen to have caught the topic of their conversation, would you?"

"Sorry, lassie. It gets awful loud in here after nine. I can barely hear meself think, let alone what anyone else is saying."

"Right. So, there's nothing you can tell me about her at all?"

"Only that she drank Guinness. Wish I could help some more."

"No worries. Thanks."

I drank my beer, which tasted more like disappointment than anything, and left the bar. I should have figured Lily wouldn't drink at her own local establishment, let alone meet anyone important there. She probably visited a different place every single night, just to be on the safe side. That was what Violet would do too.

I went home when I had finished my drink, feeling disappointed. I didn't really have anywhere to go from here. I was out of leads. But that didn't mean I was going to give up. After all, I was sure DCI Johnson would be following me again and Violet as well. I would manage to outsmart him and figure out what he was doing. I just had to be patient.

If there was anything I'd learned by going through the entire process of becoming a doctor, it was patience. I had all the time in the world.

VIOLET TEXTED ME AROUND FIVE, LETTING ME know we would meet in about an hour. I greeted Jake when he came home from work and then headed out to see if we could convince a killer to give himself up.

"So, what's the plan?" I asked Violet as we headed for the tube station. "Or is this yet another situation where you're going to keep it quiet because that's just how you are?"

"No, it is not," Violet admitted. "In fact, I believe it imperative that you know ahead of time what we are doing. We are meeting with a number of the attendees from that night. Not all of them will have had the opportunity to kill Jeremy, but everyone who did will be there. I will be accusing one of them of murder, but it will not be the one who did it. And then I will see how the chips fall."

"Is that Violet code for you have no idea what's going to happen and you're totally going to wing it?"

Violet sniffed. "I do not *wing it*, as you say. Never. I always have a plan."

"Whatever you say," I said with a smile. "No matter what happens, it's better than anything I've come up with. I still don't even know who did it."

"You will soon enough."

We arrived at the hotel where the athletes were all staying, where Kristof had been arrested a few nights earlier, the Park Plaza Westminster. Violet led us to one of the meeting rooms. When we entered, a few people were already waiting.

The room had a table at the center, surrounded by chairs. At the far end, a smaller table was laden with fruit, snacks, and jugs of water. The room's carpet was bright red, with wavy white lines running through the pattern. The white walls were intermittently broken up by wooden cabinets and artwork.

I looked around to see who was here. I immediately spotted Emily standing at the back of the room, holding a glass of water in both hands as if she just needed something to do with them. She offered me a small smile when she locked eyes with me, which I returned.

Sitting at one of the chairs, texting on his phone and not even looking up, was Simon.

Sid was in one of the other corners, gesturing while chatting on his phone, and stepping away from him was El, who almost faded into the white background of the wall in his white polo shirt and shorts.

"Thank you for coming," Violet announced, motioning for everyone to take a seat at the table. "I appreciate everybody here making the time to learn who killed Jeremy Flagstaff."

Chapter 17

Multiple people around the room looked at each other in confusion.

"Hasn't Kristof already been arrested for this murder?" Simon finally asked. "It's finished. Case closed."

"I am very glad that you asked that. No. As much as multiple people in this room wish he was guilty, he is not. In fact, I will have him join us now."

Violet went out into the hall and returned a couple of seconds later with DCIs Fletcher and Johnson, Kristof scowling between them.

"You," he snarled in Violet's direction as soon as he saw her. "I know this is your fault. You're the one who put me in jail."

Violet replied with an enigmatic smile. "Come, Kristof. Have a seat. We have come to find the guilty party for the crime you were wrongfully arrested for."

"You're going to pay for this. Don't think you can get away with putting me in jail for something I didn't do."

"I would be careful if I were you. That sounds like a threat, and here in England, threatening somebody counts as a crime. Besides, the last time you threatened me, life didn't go so well for you, did it? So sit down, and listen while I tell a story."

Kristof grumbled to himself but dragged one of the chairs out from the table and threw himself onto the seat, legs splayed and arms crossed in front of him to make it obvious he didn't want to be here.

"Good. Now, the problem with this case, as is usually the case when somebody murders a person with a lot of money, is the motive. There are always too many people after the money. Here, every person with the opportunity to murder Jeremy had a money-related reason to do so. Kristof, you were angry because Jeremy had told you he was invoking the morals clause in your contract and essentially tearing it up, costing you millions of pounds."

"Yes, but I did not kill him. You said that yourself earlier."

Violet ignored his response and continued. "Emily, you are the exception in that you had no reason to kill Jeremy whatsoever, as far as I can see."

The young Canadian had gone sheet white at

mention of her name, but when Violet explained that she wouldn't have done it, she relaxed slightly and offered up the weakest of smiles.

"Sid, however, had motives in spades. He and Jeremy were arguing about how best to approach this situation with Kristof, and the stakes were high. No matter how much somebody pretends otherwise, tens of millions of pounds is enough to kill a person over. Even if you have billions. No, I did not eliminate Sid as a suspect just because he is worth billions of pounds."

Violet paused and looked around the room. "And of course, there is Simon."

"Please. I wasn't even at the party anymore when Jeremy was killed."

"No, but that does not stop you from having a motive to kill him. Jeremy was going to tear up the contract with Kristof, which would have cost you millions of pounds as well."

"Still didn't kill the guy. Can't prove I did."

"We will see. But that is everyone in the room with a motive to kill Jeremy."

El made a small noise in the back of his throat, and Violet looked up at him as if seeing him for the first time. "Oh. That is right. I forgot. There is also Elton John. But he did not have motive to kill Jeremy. Jeremy wanted to sign him on their label once they dropped Kristof. So why would he kill him?"

"I didn't," El said forcefully.

"So, we move on. Now, on to the facts of the case. Kristof did not kill Jeremy. The evidence that he had the cyanide was planted in his apartment by a person who will remain nameless." I resisted the urge to smile as Violet continued. "However, I was informed by the police that they received an anonymous tip that Sid Miller did, in fact, purchase the cyanide. Now, that was interesting for a few reasons. For one, the caller did not leave their name. And secondly, when the police searched Miller's home and office, they found no evidence of this whatsoever. But Sid did not commit this crime."

Violet paused for a moment, looking around, savoring the moment in which every eye in the room was focused on her before continuing, letting the tension grow before she continued.

"Simon did. And Sid Miller was instrumental in proving it."

I raised my eyebrows as a collective gasp rang out through the room.

Simon's face turned to one of stunned anger. "Now you just hold on a second there," he said, bolting from his chair.

But Violet motioned for him to sit. "No, no. You do not get to speak. This is my meeting."

"Well, you don't get to throw accusations like that around willy-nilly."

"I can say whatever I want when I can prove it,"

Violet replied. "Now, sit, and enjoy your last few moments of freedom before you are thrown in jail for the rest of your life."

"Yeah, this I want to hear. They tell me you're the best detective alive, but this is total bull. I wasn't even there, so how could I have killed Jeremy? I thought you were supposed to be smart."

"Ah, but I could not come to the conclusion without the help of Sid," Violet said, looking over at Jeremy's business partner.

I still had no idea where she was going with this, but I knew Simon was innocent.

"Sid was the one who told me that there was a vial of cyanide inside Simon's office. He spotted it when the two had a meeting the morning before Jeremy was killed."

Simon sputtered, apparently unable to form even a coherent sentence.

"So ultimately, it is Sid who is the hero in this case. He is the one who gave me the information that is leading to Simon's arrest. DCIs Fletcher and Johnson will now be happy to cart him off to jail. I have already called the journalists. They are waiting outside both to get the arrest on camera and to interview Sid. His help was instrumental in bringing the perpetrator to justice."

"Wait," El interrupted. "How do you know it's real though? What if Sid planted the evidence to make it look like Simon did it?"

"Yeah," Simon said quickly. "That. I didn't have cyanide. I never bought any. That's insane."

"No. It has been proven to belong to Simon despite his objections. Sid is the one who has brought justice to this case."

"But... he can't," El said quickly. "No. Sid did it."

"That is what you believe, but the evidence points elsewhere."

"You got an anonymous phone call telling you the cyanide was at his home."

"Yes, and as I have said before, that turned out to be a prank call."

"It wasn't a prank. The cyanide was *there*," El snapped.

"How do you know?" Violet asked quietly, her eyes flashing.

"Because I put it there, damn it!" El yelled. "Don't you get it? Sid isn't some hero. This isn't his victory. He didn't do anything except frame someone else."

The room fell silent for a moment as everyone came to terms with what they had just heard, and El's face froze as he realized what he had just said.

"That's right. You killed Jeremy, with the intention of framing Sid for his murder. You wanted them both to suffer, because you overheard them in the bathroom. You told us you didn't know what they were talking about, but you did. It was you.

Neither one of them was going to sign you, and you wanted to make them suffer," Violet replied.

"Yes," El snapped back at her. "That's right. I thought Jeremy was on my side. I thought he wanted me as part of his brand. I was going to do it. I was going to show Simon that I'm not some boring idiot who can't get a contract. I was going to do it myself, and I was going to make the big bucks. But Sid kept trying to convince Jeremy it was a bad idea. He needed to go. I brought the poison to give to him. He was supposed to die. But then I over-heard them talking when I was in the toilet, and I knew they were both going to screw me over. I couldn't kill them both. That would be too suspi-cious. Besides, once one of them drank the cham-pagne, the other certainly wouldn't keep drinking. So I changed my mind. I was going to kill one of them and frame the other for his murder."

"And so Jeremy died."

"I wanted Sid to suffer. He had to rot in jail. He couldn't get away with treating me like this. Don't you get it? I'm one of the best tennis players in the world. The best!" Kristof snorted, but it went unno-ticed in the midst of El's rant. "I'm up there with the legends. Pete Sampras. Roger Federer. Arthur Ashe. I should have courts named for me. My face should be plastered on every billboard from here to Melbourne. And this was my chance. My chance to show Simon that he was a bastard for dropping me.

My chance to get a big contract, one that would make me shine. And they took it away. The deal never got signed because they decided I was too boring. Well, I showed them boring. No one ever thinks of me. Even in this conversation, I was forgotten. But now, no one will forget me."

El lunged toward Sid, throwing himself at the man, but the two police officers were faster. Next thing I knew, they had El in handcuffs, his face pressed against the table, and were reading him his rights.

"I told you I wasn't boring!" El shouted. "Everyone loves Kristof for being a bad boy. Well! Now, everyone will think of *me* when they hear the name Elton John. I'm the famous one. I'm the one everyone knows. My face will be in *every* paper."

"Yes, it will," Violet said quietly as he was led away.

The rest of the room sat in stunned silence.

"Well, I must thank you, Sid, for your help in today's activities. Simon, I apologize for the fear that I must have instilled in you, but it was imperative that your reaction to my accusation be genuine."

"I'm still not sure I even know what happened. El killed Jeremy? Really? I never thought he'd have it in him."

"Most people are capable of murder if given a strong enough motive. For El, it was the idea that he was being swept aside for someone else yet again, a feeling he felt regularly despite his success on the court."

"Yeah, well, being a tennis robot doesn't make you good at selling anything. Especially not when you share the same name with someone who's the opposite," Simon said.

"And me?" Kristof demanded. "Where is my apology?"

"You do not get one. Everything that has happened to you, you deserve. And yes, you have been released from prison here, but I imagine there are police in Berlin who would like to speak with you."

"I know you did this," Kristof snapped at her.

"Prove it," Violet dared him with a smug smile. She could do smug better than anyone else I knew.

"You're going to pay for this," he said. He jabbed a finger in her face before storming off.

"He really has not learned anything from his stint in prison," I pointed out.

"No. Not yet. But he will see. I do not think Kristof Mayer is going to enjoy his future."

"Yeah, I think you've well and truly destroyed that."

"To be fair, I simply exposed the actions he took. He was the one who ruined his own life. There are consequences to what one does."

"Like El. I had almost completely forgotten about him, I have to admit. He was the one who made the anonymous phone call to the police?"

"Yes. And of course, Sid called us in a panic because he had found the cyanide in his home and didn't want to be found guilty. He did the smart thing in coming to us. If the police had found it, then the case might have gone very differently for him."

"Well, luckily, you were on it."

"Yes. Sid is very lucky that El decided to be so arrogant as to commit his crime while I was in the room. And he very nearly got away with it. There were simply so many people who had a motive. But the real motive was not to kill Jeremy Flagstaff, it was to frame Sid Miller for having killed him."

"Either way, I'm glad this case is over."

"I am as well. And now that we have saved Sid, I imagine we will also be in line for some more free tickets to the tennis," she added with a wink.

"I'm certainly going to enjoy it."

As we were leaving, Violet excused herself. "I have another appointment with DCI Evers regarding Mortimer Gladwell. I expect she will be calling you herself tomorrow for an official statement."

"Go for it. She's working hard if she's still there at this time of night."

"Yes. I am impressed with her work ethic. She

does not fully think things through, but of course, very few detectives do. But she does try. I am finding that I'm more patient with her, perhaps due to my friendship with you."

"I'm going to take that as a compliment and ignore the insulting undercurrent."

"There is supposed to be no insult. It is a compliment. There is no one else like me, but all my life, I have expected people to be. You have taught me that I can accept people for who they are and still find that they are useful."

"I'm glad to hear it. Okay, I'm going home. I know I slept for about hours today, but I'm still tired, and I'm going to try and get a good night's sleep."

I said goodbye to Violet and headed down the street. I was about a block from the hotel when I was suddenly shoved from behind and pushed into an alleyway.

I gasped, throwing my elbow up and nailing my attacker. I heard a crack, and he swore. I paused as I recognized the voice. It was DCI Johnson.

"You're going to pay for that. And for following me. You're in the way, and you've outlived your usefulness."

I moved to run away from him, but the next thing I knew, I felt a stabbing pain in my abdomen. I looked down to see a knife sticking out of me.

DCI Johnson turned and ran, leaving me in the

middle of a random London alleyway, bleeding to death.

This wasn't ideal.

∼

Find out what happens next by pre-ordering Book 11, Knifed in Knightsbridge.

A Note from the Author

Thank you so much for reading! If you enjoyed Wiped Out in Wimbledon, sign up for my newsletter to be the first to find out about future new releases: http://www.samanthasilverwrites.com/newsletterb

Other books in this series:
Poison in Paddington
Bombing in Belgravia
Whacked in Whitechapel
Strangled in Soho
Stabbed in Shoreditch
Killed in King's Cross
Murder in Mayfair
Nixed in Notting Hill

About the Author

Samantha Silver lives in British Columbia, Canada, along with her husband and the memory of a little old doggie named Terra. She loves animals, skiing and of course, writing cozy mysteries.

You can connect with Samantha online here:

Facebook

Email

For the most up-to-date info and lots of goodies like sneak previews, cover reveals and more, join my Facebook Reader Group by clicking here.

Made in United States
Troutdale, OR
04/17/2025

30647178R00111